REUNION IN PRAGUE

RICHARD WAKE

MANOR AND STATE, LLC

SIGN UP FOR MY READING GROUP AND RECEIVE A FREE NOVELLA!

I'd love to have you join my on my writing journey. In addition to receiving my newsletter, which contains news about my upcoming books, you'll also receive a FREE novella. Its title is *Ominous Austria*, and it is a prequel to my first series.

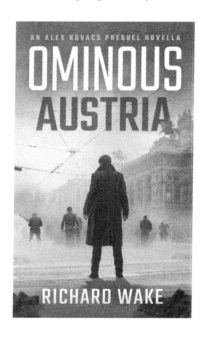

The main character, Alex Kovacs, is an everyman who is presented with an opportunity to make a difference on the eve of the Nazis' takeover of Austria. But what can one man do? It is the question that hangs over the entire series, taking Alex from prewar Austria to the Cold War, from Vienna, to Switzerland, to France, and to Eastern Europe.

To receive *Ominous Austria*, as well as the newsletter, click here:

https://dl.bookfunnel.com/g6ifz027t7

PART I

1

_____

The displaced persons camp at Ravensburg hugged the Danube, my Danube. Well, not exactly my Danube. Vienna held no illusions for me anymore, and that was true. Hell, pretty much nothing held any illusions for me anymore, a function of age and predisposition. But there was still... something. My Danube. Maybe it was as simple as the decades-old memories of teenage picnics and young lust and blankets used more for camouflage than ground cover.

This was so different. This, this camp, was neither charming nor hopeful on its surface. I guess there was hope, deep down, but you needed a pick and a shovel and a miner's lamp to find it. The thousands and thousands of people who were there — mostly Ukrainians, they said — were hoping for a ticket west, not east. Actually, everybody wanted a ticket west, but the Ukrainians were the most vulnerable to being shuttled back home, back into the warm embrace of our Soviet "allies." So there was hope, deep down below the surface, but there also was fear. That combination of emotions is what they wore on their faces — except for the kids kicking a football around, scampering in and out of the lines of laundry drying. Kids are kids in whatever the setting, and they were running themselves to exhaustion next to the chain-link fence that separated the camp from the river. It didn't seem like much of a barrier to me, but if there was a problem with escapees, it wasn't obvious. The fence wasn't even guarded during the day.

Sitting off to the side — a place where people with neither laundry nor children to worry about seemed to congregate — I spotted her immediately. It was the long red hair. I had been studying the photograph for more than a week, and the face seemed to match, but it was the hair that clinched it. Not red exactly, but reddish blackish. She was Czech, not Ukrainian, and she wasn't talking to anyone. On a bench by herself, just staring into the distance.

I walked over, asked if I could join her. Asked in Czech, my native language. Her face lit up, as I had hoped, as Fritz had predicted. Before the mission, we practiced how this might go, and he said, "You're more than 20 years older than she is, but those years should melt away when she hears a few words in Czech, lover boy."

"But there will be other Czechs there, right?"

"Some, sure. But 90 percent Ukrainians. Maybe 95 percent. And the other thing is, in those places, nobody trusts anybody. You'll see. Families all separate — other than the kids running around. Not a lot of casual chit-chat going on. So, a little Czech, a little smile — you'll see."

And so it was. I ran my hand along the bench to brush away some dust and caught a splinter. I cursed and stared at it for a second, and then the woman took my hand and angled it toward the sunlight and plucked it out.

"All better," she said. Then, she shook the hand properly and said, "Lidia. Lidia Svoboda."

"Alex Kovacs," I said, honestly. No point in lying. Nothing to gain.

"Prague," she said.

"Brno," I said, also honestly. It was where I grew up before moving to Vienna as a teenager.

"Small-town boy," she said.

"Not that small."

"Smaller than Prague."

"You act as if Prague is like New York."

"It's bigger than Brno."

"Not that different," I said.

She leaned over, got really close. She ran her fingers through my hair and then gave it a tousle.

"Looking for hayseeds," Lidia said.

I laughed. She laughed. More chatting. More flirting.

"How long have you been here?" she said.

"Just today. This morning. You?"

"Two weeks — two weeks tomorrow."

I knew that already. I knew everything I needed to know about Lidia Svoboda. It was all in the camp questionnaire and the supplemental briefing from Fritz. I had a photocopy of the questionnaire in my bag — although I'm not sure why I needed it because, after about 20 readings, I pretty much had the thing memorized.

Fritz had warned me to take my time, not to rush, not to blow it by seeming too anxious. He said that the note I should be trying to hit was somewhere between big brother and tender lover. He said, "It really works either way. You only get laid under one of the circumstances, though."

"Unless her family history..."

"Christ, don't even go there," Fritz said. "But it works either way. And you really have as long as it takes — provided, that is, that it doesn't take a month. If you haven't charmed her by then, we go to Plan B."

"Which is?"

"Which is not your concern."

"So..."

"So, just worry about charming her ass off," Fritz said.

The splinter, the hayseed. This wasn't going to take a month. It wasn't going to take a week.

We talked about the accommodations and Lidia asked, "Barracks or tent?"

"Tent," I said.

"Barracks for me — you might be better off."

"Until it gets cold."

"If we're still here when it gets cold, I'll shoot myself and you can take my spot."

"Women and men in the same barracks?"

"No — that was just a figure of speech," she said. "Just women and children in the barracks. Crying, screaming children. Like I said, you might be better off."

"Screaming children versus snoring, farting men," I said. "Might be a coin flip there."

She laughed.

I asked her about the quality of the food in the camp and Lidia said, "Not bad, surprisingly — and plenty of it." We agreed to meet that night on the line at the dinner wagon. I stood up and she grabbed my hand, and examined where the splinter had been, and held it for a second, and said, "You should wash that, just in case."

This was going to be so easy.

2

Dinner was entirely pleasant, and it was me who cut off the evening right after. Lidia would have gone for a walk if I had asked, at least a walk, but it was best to stick to the truth. That is, that I was exhausted after my arrival that morning, and that I'd look for her the next day at lunch.

Back in the tent, my cot was right below one of the window flaps. The moon was not full, but bright enough. And so, amid the snoring and the farting of about 30 grown men, I was able to read Lidia's camp questionnaire. Again.

Name: Lidia Svoboda

Age: 27

Home: Prague

Marital status: Single

Spouse: N/A

Parents: Tobias and Vera Svoboda

Siblings/Spouses: Sister Berta (married to Vilem Novak). Sister Maria (unmarried).

Education: Bachelor of Arts in Philosophy, Charles University

Desired destination: United States, for graduate study at the University of Chicago

It went on from there, but the highlights were there at the top. When I told Leon about it — Fritz knew what good friends we were and had long permitted me to consult with him — he said, "So, your job is to try to fuck a philosophy student?"

"A bit more than that," I said.

"Maybe you should go for the big brother thing instead."

"Screw you."

"You're a little too dark for a philosophy student. A little too, I don't know, mechanical."

I folded my arms and offered a fuck-you glare. Leon continued.

"Look, if the job is to romance her, I'm the man, not you."

"You act like we're in the same business. You write for a newspaper. You don't do what I do. You have no idea what I do."

"I know plenty," Leon said.

"You know what I tell you."

"Which is everything."

"Like hell."

At which point, Leon returned the conversation to his strongest suit: sex. He was and always had been a savant when it came to matters of the heart (and, particularly, matters of the undergarments). He told the story about a philosophy student from Salzburg who he met in the early 1930s and bedded within 90 minutes of their introduction.

"Fast even for you," I said.

"Just need to have a feel for these things."

"Which involved, in this case..."

"A strong drink and a single whispered word."

"Which was?"

"Schopenhauer," Leon said. "A whisper, a nibble on her ear lobe, and she was pulling up her skirt."

I nearly spit out my beer.

"And what do you know about Schopenhauer?"

"Not a fucking thing," Leon said.

"But after, she must have asked you."

"After, I was out of her flat while she was using the toilet. A wonderful memory for both of us."

I clinked his glass.

"So, I'll acknowledge that you'd be in her pants quicker than I would. But what about the rest? The part where you have to make contact with the brother-in-law?"

The brother-in-law, Vilem Novak. Also known as Captain Vilem Novak of the Czech army. We knew that because the Gehlen Organization — which employed me and Fritz, my handler — collected information from every one of the questionnaires filed at every one of these godforsaken refugee camps. It was part of the service Gehlen performed for the American Central Intelligence Agency — and the more information the Gehlen Org could collect, and the more boots on the ground that the Gehlen Org could supply behind the Iron Curtain, the more American cash Gehlen collected and the more entrenched Gehlen became as the core of the next West German spy agency.

So, the minions at headquarters read all of the questionnaires and added more and more names to the bulging card files. And every time they ran across a name like Vilem Novak, they went to the file and searched for an existing card. And, in Novak's case, lo and behold. His card said that he was a captain in the Czech army, which was moderately interesting. And that he was helping to run the Czech secret service out of a headquarters in Karlsbad, which was more than moderately interesting.

The way Fritz explained it, "Let's just say that the Vilem Novak card in the file engorged a few members at headquarters." But after the blood went back to where it usually resided, there was a great debate — "All the way up to Gehlen, to the old man himself," Fritz said.

"The old man who you're older than."

"Perhaps. But the point is, there was a concern that Vilem the brother-in-law might be sending Lidia the philosophy student to the United States as a plant of some sort."

"Like a sleeper agent?" I said.

Fritz nodded.

"Something like that. But we did some checking with our people in Prague, best as we could in a hurry, quick-quick. And from everything they were able to find out, Lidia is legit. She hates the Commies, and she left for political reasons, and she really wants to study in Chicago. She's apparently been talking about it for years, before Vilem even married the sister."

"Which means?"

"Which means, if he married into that family, well, maybe we can turn him," Fritz said.

"And the way to Vilem..."

"Is through Lidia and the rest of her family," he said.

Which was what I was doing in Ravensburg, re-reading a copy of Lidia's questionnaire by the light of the moon. Re-reading, and rehearsing what I had worked out with Fritz, and remembering the one last bit that Leon had said.

"So, Brno," he said.

A statement, not a question.

"What about it?" I said. "I'm going to Prague."

"When was the last time?"

"Prague? Brno?"

"The whole fucking country — you know, the land of your birth. When was the last time?"

"Fuck if I remember."

"Try," Leon said.

My reply was silence. I didn't want to try. It had been decades — more than two, less than three. Probably less than three. After my mother died from the Spanish Flu — 1918, Christ — I never felt there was a real reason to go back. Well, there were reasons, I guess, but there was no desire to go back.

"Try," Leon said, again.

More silence.

"Fuck trying," I said.

"If you're not going to go home, they really should send me in your place," Leon said. "I'm much better suited, and you know it. Much better suited to deflowering a philosophy student."

"And the brother-in-law?"

"He needs deflowering, too?"

"He needs convincing," I said.

"Details, my boy."

"A little more than details, I think."

"Perhaps," Leon said. "But all roads lead from the panties. I think Schopenhauer wrote that."

3

_____

The opposite corner of the camp, away from the Danube and bordering on a forest, was where the sex happened — not just for Lidia and me but for everyone. The women and children were living in the barracks, the men were living in the tents, and this patch of grass along a 10-foot chain-link fence was where conjugal relations took place.

Once it became dark, the etiquette was unspoken but obvious. It was a big field, and so the expectation was that the definition of privacy was at least a 50-foot buffer from the next humping pair. The two armed guards were fine with all of this, by the way. The two of them walked back and forth along the fence, never leaving the fence, respecting their own buffer. You and your woman brought your blanket and your bottle, picked out a spot, and commenced. Because the women took turns watching the children back in the barracks, the protocol seemed to be a chance about every third night. For Lidia and I, this was the fifth time in two weeks.

We were finished and put back together, just looking up at the stars and drinking a second glass. We had about an hour altogether — another part of the unspoken protocol — and were squeezing out every minute. The sex was fine, but the real business took place during these final minutes — the sharing of hopes and dreams and secrets. It was earlier in the week, staring at the stars, when I asked one question about her family and Lidia talked for about five minutes without taking a breath: about her stern father, her kind mother, her cynical sister Maria, her frivolous sister Berta, and about Berta's husband Vilem.

"A hunk, as the Americans say," Lidia said. "A hunk and an asshole. Lots of opinions. But we get along because he knew I hated the Communists, and he would tell me stories about his incompetent bosses."

At that point, Lidia was interrupted by a moan from the next blanket. If you listened closely, there was actually a low symphony of grunts and moans. If the wind was blowing from a particular direction, that was where the sexual concert came from. On a still night, it was everywhere if you concentrated on it. This moan was louder though — female, not male. Louder, again, again, and then a delighted wail that pierced the night — a wail followed by a new symphony, one of laughter.

I needed to get Lidia back on track but without seeming too interested. I settled on this: "Your brother-in-law and the rest, did you see him at holidays?"

"More than that, but yes," Lidia said. "Christmas, of course."

She stopped. I listened.

"That's when he told me, last Christmas. That the country would be better off without those lunkheads in charge. I loved that word, lunkheads."

I loved it, too — not that I told her. I never brought it up again, not Vilem, not the rest of her family, not lunkheads. There was no question then where this thing was headed. It was just a matter of getting the last bit right.

Fritz had warned me, "This will be the trickiest part." When he explained it, I wondered whether the sex would end up being counter-productive and if I should just stick with the big brother scenario. It was a good conversation and a tough call, but in the end, Fritz said, "It can work either way, but I think the closer you get, the better. Besides, there's every reason to believe that she'll be more of the sexual aggressor than you will."

"Because I'm such a desirable motherfucker," I said.

"Because she's alone and vulnerable, motherfucker."

"Could be both."

"If you say so."

"Humor me."

"I don't do humor," Fritz said. But he had been right. It was Lidia who had brought the bottle and the blanket the first time.

In the days since she had told me about her brother-in-law and his contempt for his Communist bosses, I began the next bit. I needed Lidia to see me talking with a Ukrainian and appearing to transact some unspoken business with him. We had already planted the guy in the Ravensburg — two days before I got there. He was a Gehlen operative working out of Kyiv and scheduled to return after this bit of a vacation. His name was Artem and he was having a swell time in the camp, taking his blanket and his bottle and entertaining two war widows from different barracks on alternate evenings. As he said, "All I can eat during the day and then plenty of luscious desserts at night."

I was meeting Lidia for lunch most days, and I began approaching the meal tent with Artem at my side. Lidia was inevitably there first, and she would see me chatting with Artem as we approached the tent. Then Artem would peel off and join some of the other Ukrainian men for a smoke.

"Who's that?"

"Just the guy from the next cot," I said.

"Ukrainian?"

"Aren't they all?"

And that was that. The second time, Lidia asked his name. The third time, she said, "So, what, Artie never eats?" My reply was a shrug. The fourth time, I could see that Lidia noticed him but she said nothing. The fifth time was when we would do it.

It was really simple. I made sure to be five minutes late, just to be doubly sure that Lidia would be waiting. And when I saw her in the distance, the little bit of stagecraft began. Artem and I were chatting a little less casually and a little more conspiratorially than before. I was leaning into his ear and he into mine. We stopped walking, and I positioned myself to peek at Lidia. She was definitely watching. I reached into my pocket and handed Artem an envelope, and he jammed it into his own pocket. Then Artem hugged me and walked away.

"What was that?" Lidia said.

"What was what?"

"What did you give him?"

"Nothing."

"What was in the envelope?"

I stared at her for a full five seconds, trying to affect a look that combined fear and resignation. One, two, three, four, five. Then I smiled, just a little, and said, "Let's skip lunch." We walked over toward where the washing was hanging and the children were playing football, and picked a bench by ourselves.

"There's something I haven't told you," I said.

She stared and bit her lip.

"It's nothing bad," I said.

"Then what is it?"

And then I told her that I was an agent working for British intelligence, and that Artem was a former Ukrainian border patrol officer with information on exactly how the boundary was being defended, and that I had the power to put him on a bus to Munich to be debriefed properly.

When we were working it out, I asked Fritz why British intelligence. He said, "I mean, why not? Besides, the whole Gehlen business involves an explanation. British intelligence is self-explanatory — and it's more Western than we are."

"We're completely Western," I said.

"I know, but just on a map," Fritz said. "Neater, simpler. British intelligence."

So, it was the Brits who were putting the Ukrainian border guard on the bus. Fine. As always, Fritz was right. Gehlen would have required an explanation, and it might have interrupted the emotional momentum building in Lidia. As it was, there was no interruption.

"On a bus? When?" she said.

"Today," I said.

Then I paused again. One, two, three, four, five.

"I could get you out," I said.

"What?"

"I could get you on the same bus."

"When?"

"Today," I said. "Three hours."

"To Munich?"

"Yes," I said. "Munich. Western sector. I don't know how you would get to Chicago from there, but..."

Lidia hugged me and began crying.

One, two, three, four, five.

"But there's a thing," I said.

She pulled back.

One, two, three, four, five.

"There needs to be a reason — a reason for my bosses," I said.

"What do you mean?"

"It can't just be because, because of the feelings I have for you," I said. Fritz and I had practiced the line and thrown out some alternatives. In the end, we decided on "feelings" and not "love." As Fritz said, "No sense pushing it."

I paused again and said, "There needs to be some operational explanation."

"What, you want me to be a spy?" Lidia said.

"No."

"Because I will."

I smiled and said, "No. We have no need for spies in Chicago. But I have been running this through my head. And, well, Vilem. I could sell Vilem to my bosses."

"Sell?"

"As a reason," I said. "From the little you have told me, he's an army officer who is skeptical about his Communist bosses."

Lidia nodded.

"You can see the potential value in that to British intelligence, right?"

Lidia nodded again.

"But I would need an introduction," I said. "And so, what I would tell my bosses is, you agreed to write me a letter of introduction in exchange for a spot on the bus to Munich."

"You want me to write to Vilem?"

"Actually, no," I said. "I want you to write to your parents and vouch for me. Then I would go see them and have them set up the meeting with Vilem. Your parents like him, right?"

"My father always says he's the son he never had," Lidia said. "Once or twice a month, on a Sunday afternoon, they sit in the park and smoke a cigar. Yeah, they like each other."

"Good, good," I said. "So that's it. I could sell that to my bosses."

"And then I'm on the bus?"

I nodded and then handed her an envelope stuffed with cash.

"For the passage to America," I said.

She hugged me again. Hug, crying, hug again. And then, right there on the bench, Lidia reached into her bag and took out a sheet of paper and an envelope and wrote the letter to her parents.

"They'll recognize the stationery," she said.

4

I hadn't been to Prague since a grade school trip, and it kind of looked the same — old mostly, buildings in desperate need of a sandblasting. Dark. Foreboding, maybe.

The meeting had been set for the astronomical clock. That was fine in that it was one of the places they took you on a grade school trip. It was right off of the big square, Old Town Square, and there was always at least a knot of tourists gathered as the hour approached. They were there to see a bunch of nothing, in both my 12-year-old memory and my current experience. It was apparently quite a wonder when they built it but now it just seemed, well, meh. The clock strikes 12 and these doors open above the clock face and statues of the 12 apostles pass through. Then a real guy up near the roof plays a few notes on his trumpet, and everybody walks away and acts as if it was wonderful — except, really, all they can think about is their search for an ice cream cone.

Which is what I was about to do, right after noon, when this kid approached me and said, "Alex?" He might have been 20.

"Alex Kovacs?" he said. His voice almost squeaked. I actually considered glancing down to see if he had wet himself but instead just nodded.

"I'm Marek," he said. Big smile this time. Christ.

"So?"

The smile wilted.

"This way, not far at all," he said, and the two of us began to walk.

The Gehlen presence in Prague consisted of a handful of local amateurs — or, as I said to Fritz when we planned this part, "true fucking believers."

"You're awfully cynical."

"Occupational hazard."

"They're quite valuable," Fritz said. "And, I mean, somebody needs to count the train cars and monitor the KGB headquarters — stuff that you're too big to do."

"I've counted plenty of fucking train cars, as you well know," I said. "Only I managed to do it without the perpetual hard-on of the true fucking believers."

"Whatever," Fritz said. "They're only going to arrange an apartment for you. After that, it's your decision how much you use them."

As it turned out, Marek had found an apartment that was just steps from the astronomical clock — up the street a bit and then a few more steps into an alley. It was a room above a tired café, The Eagle.

We walked in, and there was only one customer in the place, an old man hovering over a bowl of soup. The waiter/proprietor got up from reading the newspaper when he saw us come in. Marek nodded, the guy nodded back, and the three of us walked up a set of stairs in the back of the café.

At the top, you could go left or right. The owner pointed left and said, "That's me." We went right.

"No lock," the owner said, opening the door. "Leave a note or something in case you need some time to jerk off."

I laughed.

"I'm not kidding."

"What's your name?"

"Jan," he said. "And, really, I am going to be in and out of here during daytime hours."

The room was not a bedroom but a store room. There were boxes piled everywhere. Canned peaches. Noodles. Tomato sauce. And wedged in among the boxes was the detritus of any one-man business — chairs with broken legs, more boxes of financial records, bits of plumbing and dented pots and pans. This was where Jan threw everything that he was going to use or repair some day.

"I was lucky," he said. "When those fuckers came and did the inventory, they didn't count this as a bedroom. But I was able to squeeze one in."

A single bed. Two kind of ratty blankets. Clean sheets, though.

"You're not the first," Jan said.

"How many?"

"Six, seven." He looked at Marek.

"Six," the kid said. His tone was that of the smartest, most eager kid in the class. Christ.

We went down to the café, and Jan brought out a bottle and three glasses.

"Is he old enough?" I said.

Jan laughed. Marek's face fell. Jan poured and immediately began talking about his involvement in the underground. I never asked, but it was as if he felt the need to establish his bona fides with me, the professional spy.

"It's like this," he said. "I was actually fine with the Soviet army — I mean, they drove out the Nazis for us and that wasn't nothing, you know? But then..."

"But then they fucking stayed," I said.

"Exactly," Jan said. "And they're worse than the Nazis somehow. It seems impossible to me — I mean, those years during the war were..."

His voice trailed off. Marek had undoubtedly heard the stories before but was still fixated. He didn't have any chest hair when the Nazis left. He might not have any now, for that matter.

"It's funny," Jan said. "I was in the anti-Nazi underground too, not that we did shit. Well, I mean, we did some things — blew up some of their vehicles, set one of their barracks on fire. But, really, we didn't do shit."

He stopped, poured, gulped, belched.

"Impressive," I said.

"We all have our talents."

Another gulp. No belch.

"But this, it really is worse than the Nazis," Jan said. "I mean, the Nazis took our country, but these guys, they're taking our country and they're trying to take our souls, too. I know that sounds like high-minded bullshit, but it's how I feel."

"Not bullshit," Marek said. He looked like he was going to cry.

"But maybe a little fucking high-minded," I said, and Jan laughed. We were going to get along fine.

I asked him if he had a street map of Prague, and he found one in a drawer underneath the cash register. I needed directions to the house where Lidia's parents lived. The two of them stared at the map for a few seconds, and Marek found the street first and pointed triumphantly — again, like the kid waving at the teacher from the front desk.

"How long a walk?" I said.

"Half-hour, give or take," Jan said.

"When are we going?" Marek said.

"We're not going anywhere," I said. "I'm going tomorrow afternoon."

"But I'm supposed to..."

"You're supposed to do what I tell you — nothing more, nothing less. Exactly what I tell you. And what I'm exactly telling you is that this is a solo experience for me. Solo. Alone. All by myself. Understand?"

"But..."

"No buts," I said, and then I stared him down until his eager eyes fell. Christ.

Marek left, and I decided on a nap in my new perch. Heading up the stairs, Jan stopped me, went back to the same drawer where the map had been, and returned with something.

"Here," he said. He opened up his hand and I plucked two little foam rubber cylinders from his palm. Ear plugs.

"They work, kind of," he said.

I shrugged.

"The clock, dummy."

I nodded. And, no, they didn't work. Not even kind of.

5

———

In the end, Lidia wrote two letters for her parents. One, she said, was private and gossipy — a fact that I confirmed later when I steamed open the envelope. The other was the introduction I had asked for.

I found the apartment building easily enough. It looked like everything else in the city, a brownish stone covered in soot. My guess was that the building owners were all in cahoots because if one of them cleaned his exterior, the rest on the block would be embarrassed into doing it. United in grime, then.

Second floor, Apartment 2B. I knocked without any advance notice. It was 4.30 p.m. — after lunch, before dinner. I didn't know if Lidia's father still worked, but either way, it seemed the right spot to take my shot.

The mother opened the door. Late sixties. Older than I expected. I did my best to introduce myself in a burst of words that lasted less than 10 seconds, ending with, "I have brought you two letters from Lidia."

The mother beamed. The father, overhearing from an over-stuffed chair, got to his feet with a grunt. Hands were shaken, names exchanged. Karel and Andrea. A bottle was produced, glasses filled.

"To your wonderful daughter," I said.

"Your accent," Karel said.

"Brno," I said.

"But..."

"I haven't lived there in a while."

"But born there?"

"Born and raised."

Andrea was quiet. I reached into my jacket pocket and produced the two letters.

"Look, Karel, it's Lidia's stationery — we bought it for her last Christmas," Andrea said.

"Birthday, I think," he said.

She handed the letters to her husband. He seemed interested in feeling their weight, their heft — which wasn't much, just one sheet of paper folded into each envelope. He nodded and handed them back to his wife.

"Should we..."

"No, read them after I leave," I said.

That was the only part of the encounter that I had rehearsed with Fritz before the mission began. As he said, "Once you get to Prague, it's all going to be on you. But if you get the letter, let them read it when they're alone."

"Why?" I said.

"I just think it's better."

"But maybe, if I was there when they read it, they'd feel a bit more pressure to agree. Subtle, but it might be enough."

We talked about it, back and forth. In the end, Fritz thought that subtle pressure might work against me.

"Look," he said. "You don't know these people and I don't know these people. And if they're really simple..."

"You mean stupid?"

"I prefer simple," Fritz said. "If that's the case, then you being there when they read it might work in your favor, like you said. But if they're a little more sophisticated, and they're likely to be — city people and all — they'll know what this is all about. They know why the daughter left; they might or might not know what the son-in-law thinks about the Communists. I mean, we're hoping he's given Lidia some kind of signal that way or this isn't even happening, right? The point is, they'll have a sense. And they'll need time to digest it all. And it'll be better if they do that by themselves without you hovering."

I didn't agree, but I trusted Fritz's instincts. As Andrea fingered the envelopes, she said, "And where are you from?"

"Brno."

"Oh, yes. Lovely little city. Been years since we've been there, though — right, Karel?"

"Last year, that wedding," Karel said.

"Oh, right."

Andrea continued to hold the envelopes rather than put them down on the side table. She cradled them like eggs. Inside the one on top was my letter of introduction, which I had read before Lidia sealed the envelope, read and pretty much memorized:

Dearest Mother and Father,

The man who delivered this letter, Alex Kovacs, is responsible for me achieving my dream. I am not in Chicago, not yet, but it was through his intercession that I made my way out of the refugee camp and to my next stop, Munich. He provided me with that passage and with funding for the trip to America. I will forever be in his debt, and I would trust him with my life.

He has asked for a favor: to meet Vilem. He would like you to make the introduction. Again, I would trust Alex with my life. He shares my beliefs, and I believe that his intentions are noble. If you could vouch for him with Vilem, you would be performing a service that will make me feel as if, in some small way, I have taken a first step in repaying my debt to him, a debt that I could never hope to erase fully.

With all my love,

Lidia

I could do small-talk with anybody, but I was struggling a bit in the Svobodas' living room. All of my training from back when, as a salesman for the family magnesite mine, had given me the ability to talk forever about nothing and everything, but the silences were growing longer as I sat there. I described the Ravensburg camp, and Andrea seemed happy that the food had been plentiful. I said I had been there for about two weeks, and the look on Karel's face seemed to indicate a man trying to calculate exactly how many times this stranger sitting across from him on the divan had banged his daughter in exchange for a bus ticket to Munich.

The calculation was interrupted by the opening and closing of the apartment door. Introductions were made. It was Maria, the unmarried sister. She seemed to live there with her parents. Single, then. Older than Lidia by at least a couple years. But after a few questions about her sister, and me repeating most of what I had already told her parents, Maria stood up and raised the string bag she was carrying.

"Carrots today, for some reason — and a short line, too," Maria said. "A worker's paradise, Prague is. A worker's paradise, I tell you."

I begged off an offer from Andrea to stay for dinner and promised to visit again before I left Prague. After they read the letter, they would understand why.

6

————

I had nothing to do the next day, figuring that the Svobodas
should be permitted 48 hours with their letters and their
thoughts. So I slept late and just wandered. I had no idea
where I was within about 10 minutes such was the tangled
warren of streets in the old town. Wandering and wondering.
What if the Svobodas wouldn't give me the introduction to their
son-in-law? What then? Just camp outside his office and accost
him there? Hey, buddy, do you hate the Commies as much as
Lidia says you do? Because if you do...

It was an option. Fritz and I had not gamed it out. As he said,
"So much will depend on the facts in hand. You wouldn't be
going in if Lidia didn't indicate Vilem was likely at least warm to
the idea of working for us. But the difference between warm and
red hot is significant. Red hot, you might approach him directly,
even without the help of the parents. Warm, I'm not so sure.
Warm, you could end up dead if you've miscalculated. That's
going to have to be your call once you get there."

On the warm-to-red-hot scale, based on what Lidia said, I'd
put Vilem in the middle and maybe leaning a bit in the red-hot
direction. But there was no way to know. It was all just an

impression. The stuff he had said, the stuff Lidia had heard, might just have been the bluster of an asshole employee. There was no way to know the depth of his true feelings. In fact, as I wandered around Prague, there was only one thing of which I was certain: that I had no desire to end up dead.

As I approached a big government-looking building, I was accosted by a kid selling newspapers. Well, not accosted — but he was shouting loud enough to be heard a block away.

"The big Schein trial — read about it before you see it," he yelled, over and over. I had to admire both his lungs and his spirit of enterprise. It was a pretty smart play, and he was selling plenty of newspapers to people headed up the main steps of the building.

I bought a paper and scanned the story on the front page. The headline was subtle, as these things tended to be:

SCURRILOUS BANKER SCHEIN
BROUGHT TO JUSTICE

The picture of Scurrilous Banker Schein seemed to have been taken after a brief dance with the rubber hoses. He appeared not to have slept, and his shirt looked to have a drop or two of blood or something on the front, and one of his eyes was nearly swollen shut. His face was turned at a 45-degree angle to the camera so that you could see the size of Scurrilous Banker Schein's nose. If it had been smaller, they probably would have taken the snapshot from straight ahead but, you know. In some ways, the Commies and the Nazis weren't all that different.

The story said that Schein was being tried for bribery, embezzlement, hoarding — what? — and the splendid catch-all of "crimes against the state." The adjectives in a 10-paragraph story included the aforementioned "scurrilous," along with "chiseling," "dastardly," "thieving," and "money-grubbing." Three times, he was referred to as "the banker Schein." Twice, "Schein the Jew."

His first name was Morris.

I decided to go inside the courthouse and watch. The seats in the big courtroom were nearly all taken, and I squeezed in next to a pillar near the back. I looked around and listened to the buzz and the hubbub and realized that I had seen a crowd like this before. It had been at a boxing match. For the people in the seats — except maybe for Schein's family, wherever they were — this was sport and nothing but sport. They were in that room to be entertained.

I had read about show trials in the Soviet Union and had half an idea about what to expect. I guess I hadn't considered that they would be exported to all of the satellites, and I didn't actually know if they had been. But here in Czechoslovakia, it appeared that the embrace was complete.

A man near the front yelled, "All rise" and we did. The three judges walked through the opening in a crimson curtain that was behind their dais. They wore robes and snarls, all three of them.

"Bring in the prisoner," said the guy sitting in the middle. He must have been the snarler in chief.

A door to the side opened and Scurrilous Banker Schein was brought in. He was dressed in what seemed to be the same shirt as in the newspaper photograph. The one eye was still nearly closed. His hands and feet were shackled, and the rattling of the chains almost drowned out the loud gasp from a woman over on the far side. Wife? Mother? Daughter? I couldn't see. I could only hear the gasp, and a loud rap of the snarler in chief's gavel, and the warning he shouted, "Enough, madam."

Schein was put into the witness chair, which was over to the right of the judges and on a dais of its own, raised so that the audience could get a good look but still low enough that the judges peered down at him.

A man sitting at what must have been the prosecutor's table

stood up, his chair scraping loudly against the floor. He cleared his throat and picked up his notes, and that's when I noticed that there was no defense table.

He went on for about 10 minutes, his voice rising and falling to draw people in and then deliver a series of blows. The recitation of the charges was cursory. He only mentioned Schein's name once and only gestured in his direction one other time. Instead of specifics, the speech was filled was platitudes and red meat. Enemies of the state. Traitors to the cause. Ingrates. Obstructionists. Impediment to progress. Scoundrels. Scoundrels. Scoundrels.

The end was delivered in a roar:

"Our people are demanding one thing: the traitors and spies who are selling our country to the enemy by their grotesque avarice must be shot like dirty dogs. Our people are demanding one thing: that is to crush these reptiles."

The judges were nodding along with the prosecutor's cadence, faster and faster as he built to the crescendo. Reptiles. The audience burst into applause as the prosecutor sat down and accepted congratulations from the guy sitting next to him. The snarler in chief rapped his gavel once. Perfunctorily, and without an admonition to the peanut gallery.

After everyone was settled down, the middle judge — the others seemed not to have speaking roles — said, "Schein, what do you have to say for yourself?"

It was then that I noticed the pieces of paper that Schein was holding. Two sheets, typewritten on both sides. He flattened them as best he could, what with the manacles and all, and he began reading. You could barely hear him.

"Speak up, Schein," said the judge on the left. He did speak after all.

Schein tried again.

"May it please the court," he said, louder this time. He

sounded somehow disembodied, a zombie. There was no emotion in his voice, but monotone didn't begin to do it justice. It really was as if all of the life had been beaten out of him.

It took him 20 minutes to get through the typewritten script. During the testimony, Schein confessed to pretty much everything except the kidnapping of the Lindbergh baby in the States. It was complete, and complete bullshit — all of it.

I mean, I can do back-of-the-envelope math as well as the next person. And if what Schein was saying was true, he absconded with enough money to equal the gross national product of Albania. If his confession was genuine, he hoarded enough pork and grain to have fed Zhukov's army all the way from Belorussia to Berlin.

Bullshit. Heartbreaking bullshit. Schein's voice cracked at the end and nearly gave out completely. But he choked out the last bit.

"The monstrousness of my crimes is immeasurable," he said. "I don't consider it possible to plead for clemency. I depart as a traitor to my party, as a traitor to my people, as a traitor who should be shot."

His head fell when he was finished. It was as if the testimony had taken every ounce of his remaining strength, and then he had none. The papers fell from his hand and fluttered to the floor. The crowd stood and screamed at him, bellowing like a right cross had connected and knocked down a welterweight, and the judge allowed the yelling to continue until it petered out on its own. It was 30 seconds, anyway. When it was almost silent, there was another wail from a woman up front. Wife? Mother? Daughter?

The judge rapped the gavel.

"Madam, enough," he said.

The judge began reading from his own typewritten script. Watching him, I wondered if the stage directions were included on the pages: *Shout... Stand... Point...* Whatever he did, though, whatever he said, Schein's head remained down.

After about 10 minutes, and right after the snarler in chief said, "Death is too good for the banker Schein, for such vermin," I had heard enough. The rest of the audience was rapt, though, and it was easy enough for me to sneak out behind the pillar and get through the door without being noticed.

7

Back to the grimy building, back to the Svobodas' apartment. Andrea answered the door and looked more nervous than welcoming. Karel grunted his way out of the chair and picked up the bottle and glasses from the sideboard, same as the first time. Hard to tell.

Andrea sat down and then stood up a second later.

"A cook's work is never done," she said, with a shrug and a giggle. A nervous giggle.

Which left Karel and I to sip our drinks in silence, each trying to read the other. Me wondering what he was about to say. Him wondering how many times I banged his daughter.

"She's a dreamer, my Lidia," he said, finally.

"It's good to dream."

"Aren't you a little too old to dream?"

"Good for the young," I said. "And I'm only 50."

"Closer in age to me than her."

"About the same."

"Closer to me," he said. He gulped down what was left in his glass and poured another measure for both of us. And then he just stared at it for a while. The silence made me uncomfortable, but I wasn't sure how to break it. I had only one question — what had he decided about the letters — but he already knew that.

So, sip and silence. Sip and silence.

"Here's the thing," Karel said. "I wasn't born yesterday. I wasn't in the resistance when the Nazis were here — a wife and two kids, it just didn't seem to be the smart play. But I had friends. And I helped them here and there. Little jobs. So I get it. And I think I understand what you're about — the ability to get Lidia out of that camp, the money for her passage to America. I don't know who you're working for, but I think I get it."

"I think you do get it," I said. The truth was, I was prepared to lay out the whole business or at least a reasonable facsimile if that was what it was going to take. But it seemed that the simple acknowledgment was enough.

Karel poured again.

"Lidia was right about Vilem," he said. "We talk. He's like the son I never had. He tells me things, hope and dreams."

"And concerns at work?" I said.

Karel nodded.

"And so..."

"And so, I'll talk to Vilem and tell him to talk to you. He's a grown man, and I don't control him, and I'm not promising you anything except for that introduction. And telling him what you did for Lidia. But that's it. It's all his decision after that."

"I can't ask for more," I said.

Then I reached into my pocket and produced a sealed envelope.

"This is for Vilem," I said. "Instructions for how he is to contact me. If I haven't heard from him in three days, I'll be back here. If I have heard from him, I won't darken your doorway again."

"You're not so dark." It was a voice from behind me, a female voice. Maria.

She looked at her father and said, "Mother and I need a little space at the moment."

"What is it this time?"

"Too much paprika in the stew combined with when-am-I-going-to-find-a-husband. You know, the usual."

Karel had been sitting up in the chair, but with that, he settled back and exhaled loudly.

"A drink?" Maria said. I had been looking at her father sinking back into his arm chair. I thought she was asking him for a glass. But in the silence, I realized and said, "What, me?"

"Yeah, you."

"A drink. Sure. Where?"

Maria grabbed her coat and opened the door. I managed to mouth a "thank you" to Karel before following her out. She led me two blocks up and one block to the right. "The Wild Boar" is what the sign above the door said, except for the missing "a."

The place was full of Maria clones, women and men in their mid-thirties. I looked around and felt old, and she somehow managed to sense it.

"Relax, the bartender's older than you are," she said.

"That's a comfort."

"For what it's worth, you don't look 55."

"Because I'm not fucking 55."

"Touchy, touchy. Well?"

"Forty-nine-ish," I said.

I got a Manhattan and Maria drank straight gin. I tried to get her to talk about herself, and all I managed to acquire was a vague description of her occupation — insurance office manager — and what she did for fun: wander around the city. There was no husband, and I didn't get the sense there was a boyfriend, and that was that.

"Enough," she said. "I'm asking the questions here, Mr. Secret Agent."

I kind of screwed up my face in reply.

"That's what Papa has been calling you for the last two days. I think he's right, and I don't see you jumping up and down and denying it, so..."

"I'm neither confirming not denying."

"Wait till you have another drink."

"I'm not that easy."

"Pity," she said.

She asked a couple of questions about her sister and the camp at Ravensburg, and I repeated most of the stuff I had already told her and her parents.

"Men and women together?" she said.

I shook my head.

"Married couples?"

I shook my head again.

"Men in big canvas tents," I said. "Women and children in wooden barracks."

"Must be some, you know, goings-on."

"They had arrangements for the married couples," I said, lying. "A couple of separate huts where they took turns."

"Love shacks," she said.

I burst out laughing.

"Big line out the door, was there?"

"You might say."

"Sounds positively primitive."

"It's a primitive act," I said.

"You should write romance novels," she said.

I was hoping that I had deflected her just enough from the thought of my sleeping with Lidia. I really didn't want the family to have that impression. Even though Karel had agreed to help with the introduction, I didn't need the thing to fall apart over that.

"Are you going to tell me who you work for?" she said.

"Nope."

"Is it OK if I guess?"

"It's a free country."

"The hell it is," she said.

"Figure of speech."

"You'll be needing to work on that if you're staying."

I nodded.

"You're working for the Americans or the Brits," she said.

"Stop."

"Brits."

I said nothing.

"Ding, ding, ding," she said.

"Will you fucking knock it off? This isn't a game, and I really don't know anything about you."

"You helped my sister and one half of a transaction, and my father is helping you with the other half. Not a game, a transaction. And if I didn't approve, I wouldn't be letting you buy me a second drink."

I got the bartender's attention, and we had two more.

"What's Vilem like?" I said.

"Gorgeous jackass."

"And your other sister?"

"The kind who worships gorgeous jackasses. I'd bet money he's stepping out on her and she has no idea."

"Not a fan, then?"

"Of which one?"

"Him? Her? Both?"

"I'm a bigger fan of his, actually," Maria said. "She's just empty — in her head, in her soul. He's more honest — an asshole, but an honest asshole. And I think he really does love my father."

"And he's gorgeous, apparently."

"There is that," she said.

At that point, the conversation became more inane. We actually talked about the weather for a minute, and she stopped herself and said, "I can't do this. I'm not my fucking parents. Thirty-six year olds don't talk about the weather to fill time, except maybe when they're with 55-year-olds."

"I'm not fucking 55."

"But it begins with a five, right."

"Forty-nine-ish."

"That ish is doing a lot of work, isn't it?"

"It's doing a tiny fucking bit of work," I said. "Tiny."

We finished up and then she said, "Thanks for the conversation, but I actually am meeting a few friends."

"Pity," I said.

She clinked my glass and smiled.

8

————

The way I figured it, I had at least two days to kill and probably three. If the request to the Svobodas was significant, and it was, the request to Vilem was as big an ask as a person could make in peacetime. You know, if that's what this was, peacetime. Would he betray his Communist bosses? Would he put his life on the line — literally, and no question about it — in order to funnel information to the West? His life, his wife's life, and maybe the Svobodas' lives, too. Because it wasn't hard to imagine Vilem getting caught, and tortured in the basement of some secret police headquarters, and ultimately admitting — after his second finger had been lopped off — that it had been his in-laws who put him in contact with the evil Western secret agent. You know, me.

Of course, I would be long gone by the time some Czech sadist strapped Vilem to a metal table and retrieved a pair of rusty loppers from a hook on the dungeon wall. I was simply the negotiator in this transaction, like the closer in a real estate deal. I would get Vilem to agree and then spell out where he would collect his routine payments and where he would deliver his information, either physically or through a series of dead drops around the area. If it was by dead drop, it was as likely as not that Marek would be involved in the collections. I would like to think, though, that he would be considered too young for face-to-face hand-holding. At least, I hoped that was the case. Because he was too fucking young, and he needed to get out while he still could.

Getting out. I thought about Marek and then I thought about myself, aged 16, begging to be shipped to Vienna to live with Uncle Otto. Begging my father, who refused. Begging my mother, who eventually consented — and who somehow black-jacked the old man into agreeing.

Getting out. I became Otto's clone — although, as he explained it from his viewpoint, he and I were always the same person, only a generation apart. We were both the sons who could never please our fathers. We were the sons who couldn't imagine a life spent at a partner's desk across from dear old dad, a life of ledgers and 9-to-5 and drinks at the club before heading home to dinner with a dutiful wife and a well-mannered brood.

As Otto said this one time — we were on our third bottle at a picnic table in Grinzing: "You know, maybe I could have done it if my father had encouraged me or complimented me instead of leaning on me 24 hours a day. Maybe I could have been happy that way."

"The fuck you could have," I said.

"I don't know. A wife, a pot roast — maybe. But I, I just couldn't. So your father got the seat at the partner's desk instead of me, and I got this life in Vienna."

"Traveling, making your own hours, seeing clients, seeing... things. Living life."

"Living a different life."

"Living a better life," I said.

"Yeah, maybe," Otto said. "Most days, I think so. Most days."

We finished the third bottle and were walking toward the

tram that would take us back from Grinzing into the city. And then Otto said, "You know what I wonder sometimes? When your grandfather died, did your dad change sides on that fucking partner's desk or just stay where he was? So, which side is Ernst on?"

I was out now, wandering around Prague. I tried to walk in a different direction every time, and this day, I was in more of a commercial district by the Vltava. I walked on the street that paralleled the river bank and looked across at a high piece of ground on the other side where a brigade of men and equipment were building some sort of monstrosity. And, well, maybe it was going to be a grand work of art — but it was monstrous. Gigantic.

Getting out. I left Brno, choosing Otto's life for myself. Ernst stayed behind, choosing the partner's desk. I hadn't been back since I was in my late twenties, which wasn't yesterday. I didn't really remember most of the visits, other than the one after my mother died of the Spanish flu, and I came home after I was let out of the army to see her grave. That one stuck with me, but not the others. The last time I saw either my father or Ernst was in 1937, when Otto died and they came to Vienna for the funeral. At least, I think it was 1937. Or maybe late 1936. Christ.

I could feel my heart racing, just thinking about it. I walked into the next bar I saw for an anesthetic. Or three. Somewhere in the middle of the second Manhattan, I was able to let it go — my father, Brno, all of it. I patted my pocket and the envelope was there. It was the money for Vilem if he agreed, the down payment. It was the most valuable thing I brought to Czechoslovakia, and there wasn't a close second.

I finished the third Manhattan and called it an afternoon. Stepping outside the bar, the light wasn't that bright — but it was still bright enough. It never didn't stun me, the light when you left the bar after a bout of day drinking. You squint, and then you think for a second that you're a bit of a wastrel and feel an instant of shame, and then you think "fuck shame," and then you take your first step and realize that you're as steady as when you walked into the place. Again, fuck shame.

I wound my way back toward the astronomical clock and the rest of Old Town Square. It was never empty. Seeing as how Czechs couldn't leave the country, every holiday had to be taken inside the national borders — which meant the mountains, a lake, or the fucking astronomical clock. Or at least it seemed that way. And between the tourists and the school groups, there was always a crowd.

I stood in the middle of the square and just watched the whole whirl go by. After a few minutes, I decided that nothing quite paired with three Manhattans better than a vanilla ice cream cone. Two scoops. I was licking at it fervently and was particularly proud that I was going to get through it without having to lick my fingers clean, when a knot of pensioners — led by a man with an open guide book — followed the man as he pointed to the right.

That's when, with the human obstructions removed, I saw the big black statue in the middle of the square — something to do with Hussites or some such thing. I saw the dark pile, and the X scrawled on its base in white chalk.

9

———

Marek — who, in the back of my head, I had taken to referring to as Skippy the Spy — was my contact in Prague, after all. As such, we did need to establish a message system that was a little bit more discreet than having him bang on the door of The Eagle. More importantly, I needed a way to contact him without going to his house — the address of which I had no intention of ever knowing. It was just operational protocol. If I knew where Marek lived, and if things went bad, that information could be tortured out of me by the secret police and Skippy could be in danger.

So, a message system. I chose the simplest method because, although primitive, it worked. I had used it in Zurich back in — when was it? — 1938, and it worked then and it would work now. No reason to change.

If he needed me, he could just stroll into the middle of Old Town Square, over to the big black statue, bend over to tie his shoe, and chalk an X on the base while his body shielded him from whoever might be watching — which was nobody, not amid the general swirl of the place. And if somebody did see him, some tourist, so what? And if the somebody who saw him was a local cop, well, what was the harm? Just tell the cop that it's part of a drunken scavenger hunt of some sort, and let him yell at you and make you wipe it off, and then make another X in a couple of hours.

Because of the way the monument was built, a little lip above the base would protect the chalk mark from a rainstorm, at least for a while. But it didn't have to last forever, preserved from rain or some city maintenance worker. Both of us were supposed to check the spot every day.

If either of us made an X, the message was simple: go to a meeting that night on the Charles Bridge. Specifically, go to the St. Norbert statue on the Charles Bridge at 10 p.m.

The day after we set the protocol, I made sure to check out the Charles Bridge in daylight during one of my Prague wanders. I had been there before, on the same school trip, because those are the two things every group of tourists or school kids were required to see: the astronomical clock and the Charles Bridge. I'm not sure they would let you leave the city limits if you couldn't prove you'd seen them.

It was as I remembered: a bridge with a bunch of statues of Catholic saints on it. I was of the opinion, both as a schoolboy and as a middle-aged man, that when it came to such things, well, if you've seen one statue of a saint, you've seen them all. And as I crossed the bridge from the old town toward the part of the city that apparently was called the Lesser Quarter, that opinion was reinforced as I walked across the bridge. St. Ivo, St. Barbara, St. Joseph — on and on they went, one after the other, and, well, fine. When I came upon — in short order — St. Francis Xavier, St. Francis Borgia, and St. Francis of Assisi, I actually laughed out loud at a long-forgotten memory. It was of a schoolmate, Frankie Herzog, who asked the rest of us, "All of those fucking St. Frankies. Do you think if I told Marta Weiss that this made me a holy man, she would let me look down her blouse?"

As it turned out, the St. Norbert statue was on the far side, toward the Lesser Quarter. It was nine statues from that end of the bridge. I counted it three times, just to be sure, because I had no idea what the bridge lighting was like at night.

Nine statues. Too close. I muttered to myself, "Goddamn it, Skippy." But there was nothing I could do about it.

Still, I was nervous for the next few hours, which meant that I spent most of them in a bar — partly for the availability of the alcohol, partly for the toilet. I left at about 9:30 and started wandering in the general direction of the bridge, walking past it twice as I checked my watch.

At 9:55, on my third pass, I stepped onto the bridge. On a cloudy night, it was as dark as I had feared. The only way to tell which statue was which was to get within about a foot of it and try to read the plaque — but, given the oxidation, that was tough going. I was glad I had counted the statues. With that, I walked all the way to the far end, turned on my heel, and walked back, counting along.

Six...

Seven...

Eight...

"Right on time," Marek said, as I approached St. Norbert, the ninth statue. "I was a little worried when you walked right past it."

"What do you mean?"

"I've been following you for 20 minutes."

"The fuck you have."

"Suit yourself," he said.

I looked both ways and there were two others on the bridge, both men, both walking dogs on leashes — one in the middle of the bridge and coming in our direction from the old town, the other about three statues away coming in our direction from the Lesser Quarter. That second one, the dog took its time pissing on Saint Whoever before its owner turned back toward the Lesser Quarter. The first one reached the top of the rise, lit a cigarette, leaned on the railing and stared out at nothing for maybe 10 seconds, and then turned back toward the old town.

"Why here?" I said.

"It's safe."

"It's too close to the fucking end."

"It's not too close to the fucking end."

"The fuck it isn't."

"If you knew the fucking city, you would know I was fucking right," Marek said.

I wasn't expecting the defiance in the voice. I was expecting a supplicant, a trainee, not this.

"Too close to the fucking end," I said.

"Fuck me," he said. "All right, the Russian security police patrol the bridge at night. And on Mondays, Wednesdays, and Fridays, the two guys on the patrol walk to the middle of the bridge and look both ways and have a smoke, and then they go back where they came from."

Skippy pointed toward the old town.

"Their barracks is on that side. So, that's Mondays, Wednesday, and Fridays. On Tuesdays, Thursdays and Saturdays, the patrols are different. One guy is a completely fat fuck. They don't walk to the middle. They barely get on to the bridge. They have a smoke, and also share a nip from a flask that the fat fuck carries. And then they go back to where they came from."

"Your fucking point?"

"The hump in the bridge, the hump in the middle — they can't see over it from where they have their nip. They can't see St. Norbert. They can't see us."

"And how the fuck do you know that?"

"It's my fucking job to know that," Skippy said. The smile on his face was even more annoying than the fact that he had been right and I had been wrong.

I looked both ways again. Nothing.

"Still, we should hurry," he said. Still smiling.

"So what's so fucking important?" I said.

"I have a message from the Svobodas — they're in..."

"I already knew they were fucking in."

"Will you let me finish? The Svobodas are in, and they've contacted the brother-in-law and given their endorsement. Now, just wait."

"But I already fucking knew that," I said.

"You knew the Svobodas had agreed, but you didn't know the message had been delivered. That's an important development, important to the timing of what's to happen. And you didn't know that part."

"I assumed it," I said. "This isn't some game, and this whole fucking thing was an unnecessary fucking risk."

"There wasn't any fucking risk," Marek said.

He was still smiling.

10

The timetable at the station said the train from Prague to Karlsbad took 3 hours, 59 minutes, and the trains left hourly. I gave myself time for a delay and took an earlier train, figuring I could just wander around the city to kill time. After all, what I knew about Karlsbad could fit on a bumper sticker: hot springs. If the bumper sticker had been from the Karlsbad tourism office, it likely would have been: "Hot Springs!!!" Anyway, walking around, I might actually learn something.

As it turned out, I really only had time for a couple of laps around the station thanks to a cow that had strolled onto the tracks and became destined for hamburger outside of some-place called Kadan-Prunerov. There was the screech of hard braking, and then a thud, and then an hour of waiting for the animal control people to perform the last rites. A cushion of an hour and 15 minutes shrunk to 16 minutes. So, restroom, lap, lap, lap.

The third time around the station, I saw the car. It was a black Tatra, as expected. It was parked on the street around the corner from the main entrance to the station. As expected.

The door on the curb side was open and I leaned in.

"Do you want to go into town?" the driver asked.

"No, toward Joachimsthal."

"Get in the back."

Thus was the code fulfilled. The driver was, indeed, Captain Vilem Novak.

He didn't say anything as he drove, out of the city and into a rural, forested area. He didn't say anything but he chain-smoked like a fiend. If the window hadn't been open, we both would have been asphyxiated within a few minutes.

Ten, fifteen minutes out of town, Vilem left what was a pretty quiet road and took an even quieter turnoff — still a paved road, but barely. He lit another cigarette, opened his door, stood up, and farted stupendously. I followed him into the woods and about 20 steps to a small clearing with two stumps. We sat on them, maybe six feet apart.

"I take informants here sometimes," he said.

"Is it wise, then…"

"They're not the kind of informants who tend to come back, if you know what I mean."

I knew almost nothing about the Czech security services or the army's role in them. Vilem Novak was army. I didn't know the army was in the ankle-breaking business. Like I said, I didn't know anything. And part of me thought that Vilem looked just nervous enough that it all might have been bluster.

"My father-in-law…"

"Nice man."

"Good man, not just a nice man," Vilem said. "Good man. He has vouched for you and for your intentions. He has confidence in your sincerity, but it is dangerous to have confidence in anybody in this country, in these days."

"I understand your uncertainty. But your father-in-law…"

"I'm taking a gamble here."

Vilem stopped, took an audible breath.

"So, what do you want?" he said.

I asked if he had ever heard of the Gehlen Organization. Vilem nodded.

"Agents here and there. Not friendly agents. That you?"

I nodded.

"Okay, so..."

"We want information about what Czech intelligence is doing in West Germany," I said.

I had thought about this and figured that the truth not only wouldn't hurt but that it would be the best option. This was an intelligence professional and that was the basis for our conversation, professional to professional. I didn't tell him everything, and was a little bit fuzzy around the edges, but there was no sense bullshitting him. That would more likely than not spook.

So, I told him most of the truth. I left out the office politics bit, the part about Gehlen angling to become the intelligence agency of the newly created country called West Germany. I skipped that, and I also omitted my suspicion that Gehlen was feeding bullshit stories about bullshit Communist plans to invade West Germany to destabilize the country before it had learned to climb off of its knees.

What was left was a truth of a sort. That is, that Gehlen — when he wasn't, I suspected, gilding the conspiratorial lily to scare his way into the big job — was always in search of actual evidence of destabilizing efforts from the Soviets and their satellites. And that it stood to reason that the Czechs had agents across the border in West Germany and that those agents were working on plans to cause as much chaos as possible.

"With me so far?" I said.

Vilem nodded.

"And those agents?"

"They exist," he said.

"And those nefarious plans?"

"They also exist," he said.

"And how clued in are you to their details?"

"Very," Vilem said.

Pause.

"Very."

This was the jackpot, then. Next, the way I figured it, I just needed to listen. People betrayed their country for different reasons, but mostly two. They did it for ideological reasons or they did it for money. There were some other shades of difference but it was really those two: ideology or moolah.

Based on what Lidia had said back in the camp, Vilem hated his Communist bosses. That suggested ideology.

But then, he said, "What do I get in return?"

Bingo. Moolah.

The truth was I always liked the moolah guys better. There was less angst. It was a transaction, with each side holding a responsibility. You do this, I give you a bag of money. It couldn't be working out better.

"I have this to start, a down payment," I said, reaching into my pocket and handing him an envelope with half of the money I had been carrying.

"We would pay you well, very well," I said. "And we will pay you in American dollars or Swiss francs. Your choice."

He lit a match and looked into the envelope.

"What am I going to do with Swiss francs in Czechoslovakia? Or dollars, for that matter?"

"You save them for the future."

"Fuck the future," Vilem said. "I'm talking about now."

I tried to ignore him.

"In the future, they would be very valuable to you in Germany," I said. "You know how close it is, just right down the road. And given where you work, you'll undoubtedly know all of the safe ways in."

"I really don't — border control is a different department. They're not even in Karlsbad."

"Still, West Germany is right there when the time comes."

"Now's the fucking time," Vilem said, lighting still another cigarette. "It's got to be now. That's the deal. I give you everything I have and you get me out immediately."

I had not expected this. I guess I always knew it was a possibility, but my hat trick had suddenly turned into a goal and an assist. A current snapshot of all Czech intelligence operations in West Germany was very valuable, but it wasn't the same as having a mole in the Czech army's security branch who would provide ongoing updates for who knows how long.

Vilem stood up, walked away. Another spectacular fart, and then he came back.

"Appreciate that," I said.

I really wasn't sure how to play this. He seemed sincere enough, but I had only met Vilem an hour, 10 cigarettes and two farts ago.

On the one hand, I wasn't sure about him. On the other hand, the promise of a Czech intelligence blueprint was great and the chance that he would just vanish on me if I asked for some time to think about it might be even greater.

In the end, it was going to be a gut instinct.

In the end, fuck it. After all, it was only money and not my money.

I pulled out the other envelope full of cash and handed it to him.

"That's for my goodwill, our goodwill," I said. "That's 20 percent of the money. You could buy a house with it if you exchanged it on the black market. You get the other 80 percent after you've given me all of the information and after you've arrived in Munich."

"So, when do we do it?" Vilem said.

I pulled out a small notebook, a pencil, and a tiny torch light with a small strip of leather attached to the handle. I was able to loop the leather around my top jacket button and maneuver the light so that it shined on the notebook resting in my lap.

"Now," I said.

11

────────

I couldn't sleep after taking the night train back from Karlsbad. I was too wired, and I didn't want to drink myself to sleep. It was important to flesh out what Vilem had given me, to add the little details missing between the scratchings in my notebook. Those details weren't likely make-or-break — in fact, they weren't — but they would give life to the essential information I had written down. And the way my mind worked — maybe the way most minds worked, I didn't know — was that a few hours of sleep acted like an eraser on a chalkboard. Too much to drink, or too much sleep, would wash away those life-giving details. So, no sleep and no drink. Well, except for the half-bottle of wine that I had left in my room from the night before.

Sending the information back to Fritz would be a two-part endeavor. In other situations, I had used a radio — and the truth was, the Germans were good enough at the technology stuff, even after the destruction of the war, that I could fit a very usable radio — battery powered and with a detachable sending key — into a shoe packed in a suitcase. I still thought about the heavy monstrosities we dealt with during the war in the French

Resistance, thought about them and laughed. Lugging one of them for a few miles was an arm-deadening chore. These new radios were almost light enough that you didn't know they were in your coat pocket.

But, for this trip, Fritz decided against the radio.

"Too risky," he said.

"I'll keep the transmissions short."

"Too risky."

"But, I mean..."

"I know, I know," Fritz said. "You feel like the radio is your lifeline. But we just can't."

"But why?"

"Two reasons really," he said. "You know how we're better at making the radios? Well, we have information — not from Prague, but from Budapest and from East Berlin — that they're better at tracking them, too. It's not just those goddamned vans driving around the city with the spinning antennas on top. It's much more sophisticated — radio towers and something called triangulation. Ever heard of it?"

I shrugged.

"Yeah, me neither, not until recently. It was apparently a technique developed during the war. They catch the signal from a couple of different radio towers, and that allows them to pinpoint the source. Well, not pinpoint, not exactly — but a lot better than before. And, like I said, Budapest and Berlin. For all we know, Prague could be even more sophisticated — and the problem is, we just don't know. So, no radio. Old school."

"I fucking hate old school," I said.

But that was where we were. In truth, old school had been updated after the war with a technique revealed by a captured East German spy. Before, the way you sent a message in invisible ink involved an entire pain in the ass — and a tea kettle. First, you steamed the paper. Then, you wrote the message in invisible ink. Then you steamed the paper again to remove as many of the pen indentations as possible. Then you waited for the paper to dry. Then you wrote a regular letter or whatever with regular ink over the top — and drank about three cups of tea during the process.

The new technique was different. We ended up calling it dry writing. Fritz had provided me with a special sheet of paper that worked like carbon paper — except what was transferred was not ink but some kind of chemical. You took a regular piece of paper, stuck the special chemical paper behind it, and then completed the sandwich with another piece of plain paper. Then you wrote the secret message in regular ink on the top sheet. The chemical sheet transferred the message invisibly to the bottom sheet. You threw away the top sheet, saved the chemical sheet for the next time, and then wrote a bullshit letter to mother, or whoever, to cover the secret writing on the bottom sheet. No tea kettle required — just a half-bottle of lousy red wine.

My message consisted of two parts — first, the information Vilem provided and, second, my assessment of him and how the future would go. I included everything — the chain-smoking, the farts, my impression that Vilem was in it for the money, and his demand for an immediate escort over the border. I told Fritz that Vilem promised some additional information once he checked the files in his office, but what he had already provided was likely the best of it. The truth was, it was dynamite stuff — the names of six Czech intelligence agents in West Germany (real names and cover names) and the cities where they were located (down to street addresses in four cases). Vilem had quite the memory.

As for the exfiltration, I told Fritz that I expected the whole thing to come together in days to weeks — likely about two weeks — and that I would be handling it personally and laying low in the interim. And that was it. Actually, it was plenty. To keep it all on one page, my writing was pretty small near the bottom.

With the letter and a roll of tape in my pocket, I walked down to the Vltava River, to the bench that had been pre-selected, and taped the envelope beneath the slats on the left side. It was about 3 o'clock in the morning and chilly. I didn't want to spend too long on the bench but I did sit for a few minutes, listening to the river. It was almost hypnotic, the sound of the moving water. It was dark where I sat — the street lights on either side of the bench were broken — and I could feel the adrenaline finally starting to ebb. If I had closed my eyes, I would have fallen asleep — but I forced myself to my feet.

I had no idea how it would go after that — with Vilem, or the escape over the border, or even the fate of the envelope that I had taped on the bench beneath my ass. I didn't know if the letter would go straight to Fritz or to Gehlen headquarters in Pullach, outside Munich. I didn't know who would carry it out of the country. I didn't know who would read it on the other side or what the reaction would be. I didn't even know who would be picking it up from the bench along the Vltava. Probably Skippy, though.

12

J ust as I had taken three laps around the train station in Karlsbad, I took three around the big station in Prague. I was killing time in Karlsbad. I was trying to decide in Prague.

Decide: go to Brno or not?

Vilem had sent a new message. We would meet again to talk in three days. That was a lot of time to kill in the store room above The Eagle, a lot of time to wander around the city. A lot of time to get drunk, to be honest. And the thought of Brno kept popping into my head.

It was the house, oddly enough, that I wanted to see. The house where I grew up and the grave where my mother was buried. My father, well, I was pretty sure he was dead. My brother, Ernst — for all I knew, he lived in the house now. I wasn't sure, and I really had no desire to see him. But it was the house. I don't know. The house.

That was what I debated as I circled the big station. The trains left once an hour — I'd already checked — so availability of the three-hour excursion wasn't an issue. But did I really want to? And what if I did end up seeing Ernst? And what if my father wasn't dead? That was probably the one that bothered me the most. My brother, I could handle. The old man, I wasn't as sure.

But, well, if I didn't go now, then... when? I was age 50 and in a line of work where people took the occasional shot at me. You couldn't visit Czechoslovakia on a whim anymore, and that wasn't likely to change anytime soon. You couldn't just go there, and I was already inside the country, and...

I tried to zone out during the train ride. I bought a sandwich and a bottle of beer in the station, and they were gone within an hour. I really tried to just think about nothing, to listen to and be distracted by the static in my head. It was easier than I had expected, too. I was half asleep when the conductor began bellowing, "Last stop, Brno," as he walked up and down the hallway outside the compartments.

It was a 15-minute walk from the station, a walk I did from memory. Right out of the station. Right again on the street after the library. Then a long walk, away from the built-up part of the city and into one of the residential parts. Then left on the street that paralleled the Svratka River. Then straight that way until I saw it in the distance. It looked smaller to me somehow but, as I got closer, I saw that none of the details had changed.

There was still the weeping willow tree in the front yard, the one that dropped the whips with which Ernst and I used to savage each other, raising welts on whatever bit of skin was exposed. The flagstone walk led up to the stone porch, still painted red. The house was a Dutch colonial, of all things — and when I thought about it, one thing was different. It was painted white when I lived there but it was a kind of dirty pale yellow now. The shutters were still black. The pillars holding up the porch were still white. If it was the same in the back, there would be an immense lawn that sloped down to the river bank, and a small dock where a rowboat was tied up.

I stood there on the sidewalk and just drank it all in for a few seconds. Maybe a minute, maybe more. For some reason, a picture popped into my head. It was of my mother, wearing a blue dress topped by a white apron, standing on the porch and ringing this big school bell acquired for one task, the one she was performing now. "Dinner," she shouted. Once, twice — and then back inside, confident that Ernst and I would have heard her and were on the way back from whatever had been that day's neighborhood mischief.

My reverie was interrupted by a female voice. Not my mother's.

"Can I help you with something?"

She was standing on the porch, wearing a sweater and rubbing her hands together for warmth even though it wasn't a cold afternoon. I walked up the flagstone path and got to about 10 feet from the porch. I removed my hat and introduced myself as Alex Kovacs.

"I grew up in this house," I said.

"The Hlavas live here now," she said.

Well, that answered one question.

"I haven't lived here since I was 16," I said, trying to prolong the conversation. The old lady's body language pretty clearly suggested that she wasn't going to let me in, and I wasn't sure what to do, so I just tried to keep talking.

Then an old man pushing a wheelbarrow came around the side of the house. He looked at me, standing there and holding my hat, and he looked at the old lady on the porch, and then he looked at me again, and then he left the wheelbarrow and came closer.

"My God, it's not you Alex?" he said.

I smiled.

"My God, Willy, you just made my day."

Willy had been the landscaper/groundskeeper/caretaker when my parents owned the house, and I guessed he was still attached to the place. He was kind of a big brother to me, even though he was as old as my father. He was the one who showed me how to bait a hook, how to row the boat. He gave me my first cigarette and howled at my choking. I thought he put something in it to make it taste extra bad, and I'm forever grateful. I hadn't had five cigarettes since.

We hugged, and he cried a little. We looked at the old lady, and she very obviously wasn't budging. I saw it and Willy saw it.

"I'm just going to take him around back, down to the river," Willy said. "Ten minutes, maybe 15."

"Don't be 16," she said.

Willy nodded then turned his head to me, "Fucking bitch. Of course, that's a terrible thing to say about my wife."

He looked at me, and we both howled.

"You know your father's dead, right?" he said.

"I figured."

"Six, no seven years ago now. Heart attack."

"He used to joke that he was the one who gave the heart attacks, not the other way around."

"Two things can be true at once," Willy said, with a half-laugh. "Come on."

We started to walk down the length of the big lawn, which was in even better condition than when we were kids. Taking care of it really was almost a full-time job.

"So who lives here now?" I said.

"Lawyer and his cow of a wife. No kids. Both assholes."

"But what about Ernst? My father had to leave the house to him."

"He did, and Ernst couldn't sell it fast enough."

"Never moved in?"

Willy shook his head.

As we got to the river bank, Willy led me to the left, to an area just in front of where the woods began. There were two gravestones there, light gray marble, one a lot more weathered than the other. My mother's was from 1919 and referred to her as "Loving Mother." My father's, much newer, referred to him simply as "Father."

We stood there for a minute, me holding my hat at my side, Willy holding his over his heart.

"No 'Loving Wife,' no 'Loving Husband,'" Willy said. "I always wondered."

I knew some of that story, but didn't feel like telling it. So I just shrugged. And then, after a few more seconds, I was suddenly overwhelmed by emotion — not crying but like a gut punch, and not only for my mother. That surprised me but...

We started walking back toward the house.

"And my brother?"

Willy sniffed.

"Still in town."

"Still married? Still with the kids?"

Willy shrugged.

"Ever see him?"

Shake of the head.

"Then how do you know?" I said.

"He still runs the mine. I mean, I've seen him from a distance — you know, on the street. But we haven't talked since, I don't know, since your father's funeral."

"Why not?"

Willy sniffed again, shook his head.

"You know your brother," he said.

PART II

13

"You know, he's really fucking furious," Ernst said.

"When isn't he really fucking furious?" Alex said.

They were standing on the edge of the train platform waiting for the Vienna express. Their father remained back on the dark green wooden bench near the waiting room.

"It's only three weeks," Alex said.

"He didn't want three minutes," Ernst said.

"Thank God for mother—"

"Did you see them at breakfast?"

"Quiet, yeah."

"Quiet, my ass," Ernst said. "Frosty. Fucking icicles could have hung from the chandelier."

Alex was 16, old enough to be out at night with his friends, not like in the days when he and Ernst used to sit on the stairs and try to eavesdrop on his parents' arguments. But Ernst wasn't quite 14. He was still likely sitting on the same step a lot of nights, three from the top.

"I still don't know how she convinced him," Ernst said.

"All I know is that she did. I'm not asking any questions."

"You know, he really fucking hates him."

"Otto?"

"Yes, Otto," Ernst said. "Like you don't already know that."

"He never talks about him."

"At the office, he does."

"And what does he say?"

"His favorite saying?" Ernst said. "That would be when he opens Otto's monthly expense report and mutters to himself, 'That fucking grifter...' I'm not sure if I am meant to hear or not. Sometimes I think so, sometimes I don't."

"And how is that seat on the other side of the partner's desk?" Alex said. "Can you smell his farts? Do you like the smell?"

"Fuck you," Ernst said. "It's only two days a month. He got permission from the headmaster."

Alex was dressed for travel — tweed jacket, sturdy shoes. Ernst was dressed for the office — blue suit, polished black brogues.

"And today is one of the days," Alex said, theatrically taking a step back looking him up and down. "I'll pretend I can't see your hard-on."

"Fuck you, asshole," Ernst said.

A train whistle sounded twice, and they looked to their left. The Vienna express was about a minute out of the station. Alex took a peek over his shoulder, and his father had not moved from the bench, head buried behind his newspaper.

"What is Otto's place like," Ernst said.

"Not sure. An apartment in Vienna is all I know. He said I would have my own room. Other than that—"

"And what are you going to do?"

"He's going to show me the city," Alex said. "And I'm hoping he's going to show me that not every adult male in the Kovacs family is a complete dickhead."

"Sounds like a waste of time."

"It's a holiday. It's an adventure. Don't you ever want to have an adventure?"

"Of course."

"And yet," Alex said. "And yet, your biggest adventure today is going to be sharpening a handful of pencils for the old man so he can write in that ledger in his tiny little hand and pretend the facts and figures somehow add up to a life."

"I'm too young for an adventure and you know it," Ernst said.

"You're not too young to have a fucking imagination."

"I have a fucking imagination."

"And the image you covet more than any other is that seat on the other side of the partner's desk. Your life is all set, and it's still a few weeks until you turn 14. Congratulations."

The train whistle blew again.

"Fucking congratulations," Alex said.

The train pulled up, and Alex reached down for the suitcase. He turned and saw that his father had put down the newspaper. He was walking slowly toward his two sons, and they both waited.

"You have your papers?" he said.

Alex patted his breast pocket and felt them. He nodded.

"Okay, then," his father said. And then the old man turned, and spoke directly to Ernst, and said, "Okay, let's not be any later than we already are."

The two of them turned and began to walk away as Alex stood there outside the train holding his suitcase. Alex watched them. Ernst turned once to look over his shoulder at his brother as the distance between them grew. The old man never did.

14

The man running the bottle shop in the Brno station was a skilled practitioner in the art of train drinking.

"Yes, sir, I can open the bottle for you... Certainly, I have cups. Paper cups. No charge. I'll give you three, just in case, because they can wilt over time, you know?"

I knew. And I appreciated the care he took because I did need all three of the flimsy paper cups to finish the bottle. And finishing the bottle was my task on the ride home — finishing the bottle and trying not to be overwhelmed by my emotions.

I was the only passenger in the six-seat compartment when we left Brno and for nearly two hours until an old woman trundled in at Pardubice. I offered her a paper cup and a bit of the Bordeaux — you know, I was nothing if not a polite drunk — but she waved her hand and took a battered silver flask from her bag.

"Experienced traveler," she said, taking what I would describe as a polite swig. Well, as polite a swig as you can take when you follow it up by wiping your gob on your sleeve.

Halfway through the bottle, the roughest edges of my emotions had been sanded away. Christ, those headstones.

Seeing the house from the outside had been nice, and talking with Willy again had been a net plus. But, those headstones.

I had expected to cry for my mother. I had not expected the rest of it, the gut punch when I saw my father's grave. I had spent all of my adult life hating him, and for good reason. I was just returning the favor. And if it wasn't hate coming from his side, not exactly, it was the kind of pernicious, unrelenting disappointment that toed close enough to the line as to be indistinguishable.

I knew I had been right to leave Brno and never regretted it for a second. Literally, not for a second. He had driven me out, and I left, and I had the better life because of it, and that was that. Literally, not for a second.

So, why the gut punch?

It was why I didn't stay to see Ernst — that and the whole danger of the thing, of being in Brno. All I needed was for some security cop to ask to see my papers while I waited in the station. I mean, I had some, but they were the old Alex Kovacs papers from when I had been a bank president in Zurich before the war. I was working for Czech intelligence at the time — the old Czech intelligence. I was running a little boutique bank called Bohemia Suisse as a cover for my work trying to figure out when the Nazis were going to attack France. All of these years later, it was hard to know if the papers would hold up — and I had no explanation for why my passport didn't have a Czech entry stamp. So, hanging around in train stations for extended periods of time was just a bad idea. Ernst would have to wait.

The train arrived in Prague on time, right at 9 o'clock. I walked back to The Eagle in a drizzle. Coming through Old Town Square, there were still several small groups milling around. Still buying ice cream. I decided to treat myself, and then I looked to my right. Christ. Another fucking X on the base of the black statue. The other X had faded, but not completely. The new one was just to its right.

I looked at my watch. 9:45. I just had time to make it back to St. Norbert.

As I approached the Charles Bridge, I saw two guards sharing a smoke. One of them was noticeably fatter than the other. Sharing a smoke and passing a flask back and forth. Skippy had been right. I stood off in the distance, and watched them, and checked my watch. 9:55. 9:56. 9:57. And then, finally, the fat one screwed the cap back on the flask and the two Russian soldiers stepped off of the bridge and turned left, apparently heading back to their barracks.

I made it to the statue right on time. Marek was already there.

"Did you see them?" he said.

"See who?"

"Fat and skinny."

"Don't know what you're talking about."

"You're a lousy liar — bad trait in a spy."

"Your grin is obnoxious."

"Can't help it."

"And now who's the lousy spy," I said.

"You want the message or not?"

"Shoot."

"Your boy says he is unavoidably detained — some kind of out-of-town mission that he can't get out of. It's going to be at least another week on top of the three days he originally said."

"Fuck me."

"What the problem?"

"Time isn't our friend," I said. "Every day I'm in this city is a day I'm in danger. Not, like, mortal danger — but you never know who sees what. Every day here is another day I can get caught, and every day we wait is another day for Vilem to change his mind."

The truth was, I didn't really think there was a lot of danger. I had slipped into the country unseen, and the storeroom above The Eagle seemed to be secret enough, and I hadn't noticed anyone taking even the remotest interest in me on the days when I wandered around Prague, or on the train to Brno. I was taking all of the right precautions, and I really felt fine about things. Still, another week — 10 more days in total.

"You worry too much."

"The day you stop worrying is the day you get caught," I said. Marek stared at me.

"Old spy proverb?" he said.

"Don't make fun of it. Heed it."

15

I was drunk enough when I got on the train that I stumbled up the steps going in, and then again in the hallway outside the compartment. At least it was empty.

The night train to Brno, then. Drunk. It was the only way I was going to do it. I didn't want to see Ernst but I had to see Ernst, if that made any sense. What kept coming back to me was that this really might be my last chance — like, ever. You turn 50 and the "like, ever" conversations you have with yourself become more insistent. Still, it took a half-dozen Manhattans to silence all of the doubts and point me in the direction of the station.

As it turned out, I slept almost the entire trip. When I woke up, I had a sore throat, undoubtedly from snoring with my mouth wide open. It was 2 a.m., and I was oddly awake — still drunk but awake. It was when I emerged into the Brno station that the flaw in my drunken plan revealed itself. I wanted to get a room and a shower before heading to see Ernst in the morning, but I was going to have to show my passport at whatever hotel I checked into, no matter how down-market. Rules were rules in a Communist country, and the hotel passport rule was pretty much ironclad. I guess I could try to bribe the overnight desk clerk — they likely turned a blind eye to all manner of tawdry shit as if it was part of their job description — but , well, ignoring sex in its many permutations was one thing, but breaking the rules promulgated by the Czech security services was another. For all I knew, the desk clerk would take my money and be on the phone to the bad guys as soon as I started climbing up the stairs to my room.

So, I realized, a hotel was out. That left me either to wander the streets for the next four or five hours or to sleep in the train station on one of the benches. As I drunkenly calculated, I tried to figure the worst-case scenario — and concluded that walking the streets was the absolute worst case. Because to get stopped by a cop on the streets of sleepy Brno at 3 a.m. was to invite a request for my papers. That just wouldn't do. Frankly, it would have been the same if I had been stopped in the station at 5 p.m. during a random check of all passengers. My papers, they just had that fatal flaw — no entry stamp from the border crossing.

But in the station... in the middle of the night... maybe.

The way the Brno station was laid out, there was a massive clock in the middle along with four boards displaying train departure and arrival times. One board faced in each direction. Along one of the long perimeter walls were the ticket windows. Along the other long wall, there was a restaurant and a few small shops, including my new favorite bottle shop with the free paper cups. Much of the rest of the space was filled with benches that faced each other in pairs — wooden, massive benches with a goodly percentage of the shellac worn off.

I looked around and saw two other men in the station. They were on facing benches, kind of in the middle, not too close to the doors that led outside. The more I thought about it — again, still very much drunk — the whole idea of safety in numbers made some sense to me. The other part of the equation had to do with the time. The way I thought about it, there was little to no chance that the Czech security service would be trolling the train station from, say, 2 a.m. to 6 a.m. If there was any kind of police presence, it would be a beat cop. And if I joined my two sleeping brethren, who might very well be regulars, well, it might just work out fine.

With that, I walked over and joined them. One was asleep, sitting up. The other was nearly horizontal with his eyes open. Glassy eyes. I sat on the other end of the bench with the sitting-up-sleeping guy. And pretty soon thereafter, I joined him in slumber. We must have made for one farting, snoring, stinking threesome. At least my clothes were clean.

At 5:30, I was awoken by what turned out to be the sound of a wooden night stick banging on the wooden bench.

"Rise and shine, sleeping beauties," said the voice attached to the night stick. It took a half-second for my eyes to focus, and then they did, and I smiled. A beat cop.

"Out, now," he said. "And I'll be checking the toilets in five minutes, so don't even bother trying to hide in a stall. A quick piss and then gone — got it?"

"Yes, yes, officer," my bench mate said. The whole dance seemed pretty well practiced.

I got to the bathroom while the two of them were still pulling themselves together. A face wash with unusually cold water oddly did wonders. Eggs, sausage, toast, and coffee from the station restaurant did even better. I felt almost human as I began the long walk to the mine. I guessed it would take an hour, but it was more like an hour and a half.

I checked my watch as I approached the gate. It was 8 a.m., and the entrance was quiet except for two guys sprinting in to get their time cards punched before the two-minute grace period was up. At least, it was a two-minute grace period when I was a kid. I asked my father once, why two minutes? And he said, "Because one minute would make me look like an unforgiving asshole."

The sign over the gate — "Kovacs Mining" — was the same as I remembered. Faded a bit but the same. I checked my watch again. If past was prologue, Ernst had already been inside for at least a half-hour. But, well, one more cup of coffee wouldn't hurt. I had it in the canteen where most of the workers stopped before starting their shifts, and I spiked it from a pint bottle of rye I had purchased from the shop in the station after breakfast. Bottle in the right coat pocket, paper cups in the left. In the end, I had to force myself to turn right out of the canteen — toward the mine entrance — and not left. As it turned out, the office was in the same place, the first building on the left.

I walked in, and there was a receptionist. As before. Not the same one, though, who had already been old in 1915. This one was young and perky. I asked to see Ernst.

"Do you have an appointment?"

"No."

She made a face, a sad face, the kind of sad face a perky young girl might make if they told her they didn't have any more chocolate ice cream.

"Who should I tell him is calling on him without an appointment?"

"His brother," I said.

At which point, she offered me a chair with half of an excited squeal — you know, like they had pistachio ice cream instead. She left me in the waiting area, knocked twice on the closed door, and entered without a word from inside. About a minute later, the door opened.

Ernst. He just looked at me, and I looked at him. He was different — older, obviously, but also much thinner. The look on his face was almost one of bewilderment. I had stood when the door opened, and he was looking up and down, from my shoes to the top of my head and then back again.

It was all very awkward. I didn't move and neither did he. No hug. No handshake. We were 10 feet apart and neither of us was doing anything to close the distance even to 9 feet.

"Well," Ernst said, and then he turned on his heel and walked back into the office. Seeing as how he didn't slam the door behind him, I took that as an invitation to follow.

16

———

Happy Heidi — that was the receptionist's name, Heidi — brought in coffee and biscuits and floated out of the office and closed the door. We sat in opposing wing chairs on either side of a small coffee table. The office was a suite, and this was the meeting part of it. Behind Ernst, filling my vision was the big battleship of a partner's desk. One side was completely empty, devoid of any paperwork.

I thought about sitting there on the empty side. I pictured myself, my younger self, sitting there in a dark suit with a ledger open in front of me and the goose-neck desk lamp shining down on it, the circular splash of light illuminating... well, what? Christ, I shivered just thinking about it.

And Ernst said, "Just passing through?"

"Sort of."

"You could have called ahead."

"It was last minute."

"Still," he said. And we sipped.

I saw the big desk, and I saw the vision of my father, and I remembered the last time we spoke. I'd already fled Austria on the night of the Anschluss and essentially turned what had been a part-time job assisting the old Czech government with some minor courier and espionage work into a full-time gig. I actually didn't have much of a choice. In order to get some resettlement assistance for myself and my friends, I had to take on the position as president of Bohemia Suisse in Zurich and become the Czechs' eyes and ears there on the eve of World War II.

Anyway, that was when my father and I last spoke. He had pretty much cut me out of the will, but I had badgered him into sending me a check for about one-ninth of the value of the company in exchange for my going away for good and not contesting things when Ernst was given the company after the old man's death. I thought it was one-ninth, but it might have been more. Or less. I honestly didn't remember anymore.

Well, then the Nazis came to Czechoslovakia in 1938 — and, just like that, they took the mine from my father. And then, while I was in Zurich, he had the nerve to call me and ask for the money back. It was a long, painful conversation — he played the honor card, and he played the guilt card, and he played the family card, and he did it with all the skill of a master manipulator. But in the end, with the money in my bank account and a safe distance between us, I pretty much told him to go fuck himself.

Last words, then. Christ.

"I can't believe you kept the money," Ernst said. It was eerie how our minds had both gone to the same place.

"Because it was my money."

"But the circumstances changed."

"Which wasn't my fault."

"But which you should have understood."

"Said the guy who stood to inherit the entire business as the younger son, completely cutting out the older son. I mean, with love, fuck you and fuck your changed circumstances."

His face got red and he leaned forward. Part of me thought

he was going to stand up and take a swing at me. But almost as quickly as the emotions flared, they ebbed. Ernst sat back in the chair.

"It's still your mine, it seems," I said.

"The fuck it is."

"The name is still over the gate. The men are still clocking in. The trucks are running. That goddamn stench from the mine is still hanging over everything."

"As you know, the Germans took everything, pretty much, and let us run it," Ernst said. "Me and Papa, employees of the Nazi state, answering to some colonel with a fucking monocle. Zimmer. Colonel Franz Fucking Zimmer. They took 100 percent of the output for their war machine and 100 percent of the profits. They took actual ownership — we had to sign the papers, right at this little coffee table — and we made a salary, that was it. And it was a shitty salary — more than the laborers, but not a lot more. We barely got by. But now the Nazis are gone, and I guess you're right. For the last five years, it's been mine. And now, well, I guess it's still mine. You know, today."

"Meaning what?"

"Meaning, we're going to be nationalized any week now," Ernst said. "That's what I figure. When Heidi knocked on the door and said someone was here, I figured it was a Commie with a slide rule and a contract I was going to have no choice but to sign. They've taken the coal mines already — did that early on, maybe 1946, 1947. The steel mills, they were taken after that. They're coming for us soon. Maybe any day now. Probably any day now. I'm sure they're just working their way down some list."

"It's…"

"It's ironic, I guess," he said. "First the Fascists take it. Next, the Commies are about to take it. Two distinct ideologies, two completely opposed ideologies, both following the same path, both ending up in the same place. Up my ass.

"It's a good thing Papa's dead — he couldn't handle it again. It really killed him the first time. I firmly believe that. He just had this rage inside of him. I bitched out loud, a lot, and we really did nearly fucking starve, but he kept a lot of it bottled up."

"He never kept it bottled up when it came to me," I said.

"This was different. This was a force that he couldn't defeat, and he knew it. He just sat there," Ernst said, pointing at the desk, "and he sat there, and he stewed in all of it. He seethed. And at the end of the day, he put on his coat and went home and seethed some more in that big empty house by himself. Seethed and drank."

"He never used to drink — maybe a wine with dinner," I said.

"That changed," he said.

Happy Heidi knocked and opened the door and asked if we wanted more coffee. Ernst shooed her away, and she closed the door quietly.

"I swear that when they wrote up the death certificate, that should have been the cause of death," he said. "Name, age, date of death, cause of death: Colonel Franz Fucking Zimmer."

Ernst stood up and walked over to pick up a bottle and two glasses from a sideboard.

"Too early?" he said.

I shook my head. Not too early.

17

"So, seriously, what the fuck are you doing here? And where did you even come from?" Ernst said.

I took a sip. It was nice, smooth.

"What is this?" I said.

"Scotch."

"Very nice."

"Single malt."

"And how did you get that in the great workers' paradise?"

"Papa had a case in the basement of the house. This is the last of it."

Another sip.

A long pause.

"Well?"

"Well what?"

"Are going to tell me what the fuck you're doing here or not?" Ernst said.

I had thought about the question beforehand. It was about the only piece of the conversation that I had rehearsed ahead of time. I settled on the lie that I was now affiliated with a steel manufacturer in Koblenz, West Germany, and that the company might or might not start doing deals with the Czech government for coal and a little bit of iron ore.

"How is that possible?" Ernst said.

"What do you mean?"

"West Germany, Czechoslovakia. West, East. How is that possible?"

"The dirty little secret is that your Communist overlords, for all of their purity of heart and strength of ideology, still need Western currency to make the whole socialist paradise thing run. They need German marks and Swiss francs — especially Swiss francs — to pay for all of the shit that isn't grown here or manufactured here. So..."

"But you never hear a hint of that."

"And you never will. But, well, I'm fucking here, aren't I? There's your hint."

"How big is it?"

"It isn't anything yet, not officially. Just dipping a toe."

"And what's your role?"

"Same as it ever was — schmoozer in chief," I said.

Ernst laughed. It seemed genuine.

"Otto and Alex, brothers in bullshit," he said. "The highlight of my month used to be when the two of you sent your expense reports. Papa insisted on opening them himself, and then he would turn three colors when he read them. It's the only time I ever heard him curse — except for a time when he hit his thumb with a hammer."

"You have to spend money to make money," I said.

"Otto teach you that?"

"Among other things."

We sipped. Ernst seemed more relaxed.

"Wait — Koblenz?" he said.

"Yeah," I said.

"The Gnome?"

"Unfortunately dead. His son runs it now. Normal size human being, alas."

The Gnome was my nickname for Evald J. Gruber, the man who owned the steel mill. I used to dine out on my stories about the Gnome. Half of my job as a traveling sales rep for the mine was to deal with delivery issues and other complaints, and to extend contracts and whatnot. The other half was a social function — anything from dinner or drinks with the client after the meeting to, well, anything. In the case of the Gnome, who was five-foot-nothing and about 70 years old, my after-meeting task was to arrange an assignation for the him. His taste ran to six-foot amazons. Actually, two of them at the same time.

"And the son?"

"Not even a cocktail after work," I said.

"Nothing's the same anymore, is it?" Ernst said.

It was all a lie, of course — the steel mill, the Gnome's son, all of it. I could still amaze myself at the ease with which I could embroider an entire story and make someone believe it. As Ernst poured us each another measure of the single malt, he cracked himself up recalling the time I got a picture of the Gnome being lifted into the air by the two girls as they swung him out the door of the bar we were in. I laughed, too, and wondered whatever happened to that snapshot. Ernst was right. Nothing was the same anymore.

"Married?" he asked

"I was. She died. The war."

"Kids?"

"No," I said. And I was hit by the quickest wave. When Manon died trying to escape from Lyon in a plane piloted by the French Resistance, the crash also killed the baby she was carrying. My baby.

"And you? Still married?"

"Yep," Ernst said. "And two kids, girl and a boy, 12 and 10. They fight like we did."

"Not likely."

"Very likely. The girl is older and she just tortures her brother. I mean, it's almost sadistic sometimes. She did something about a month ago that I swear you did to me."

"For the record, your honor and members of the jury, I deny everything. And besides, I'm sure the statute of limitations has run by now."

"The hell. You can't deny this one. You pissed in my bed for three days straight while I was brushing my teeth in the morning. Devious prick. And after we went to school, Mother found the wet sheets. By the third day, she was all worried I was sick or some shit. And I told her I had no idea what she was talking about, and they didn't believe me. And then, when I was asleep the next night, you stuck my hand in a bowl of water and I really did piss the bed."

I saw laughing semi-uncontrollably at that point.

"Motherfucker," Ernst said. "She dragged me to the doctor the next day, and he talked her off the ledge. But the next move was going to be a psychiatrist. Motherfucker."

"And your daughter, did she actually..."

"Piss in his bed? No. Not so devious — or disgusting, thank God. But she put his hand in the bowl of water so he pissed the bed himself."

He was laughing even harder than I was. And then, almost as quickly as the emotion came, it went. Ernst sat back in his chair and took another sip.

18

A belch. A sigh. And then Ernst leaned forward in his chair, and punched the air with his index finger, and said, "I can't believe you kept it."

The money, again. Always the money.

"It was one-ninth, or whatever, of what was rightfully mine, nine-ninths of it," I said. "Oldest son, primary heir. And even if we ended up splitting it—"

"Out of the goodness of your fucking heart? Yeah, right."

"Even if we ended up splitting it," I said, "I still ended up with a fucking sliver of what I deserved. A fucking sliver."

"And we ended up with nothing. I ended up with nothing."

"Your miscalculation, not mine."

"And how exactly do you calculate that Hitler is going to overrun your county and take your business from you? Where do they teach you that? Where is the chapter in the business school textbooks about Nazis?"

"You screwed me and then you got screwed," I said. "Perfectly symmetrical. Entirely fitting."

"Fuck you and fuck your symmetry," Ernst said. "We were

fucking dying here. We needed that money — not to get rich, to survive. It would have made all the difference."

"So, if I'd given it back, the old man wouldn't have sat at home at night, seething and drinking, drinking and seething? Fuck you. That's a fantasy and you know it."

Ernst was on his feet at that point. He walked over to the big desk, looked down at a piece of paper, rearranged something. Then he walked back to where I was sitting but he didn't sit. He stood there, towering over me. I almost stood up as a reflex but decided against it for some unknown reason.

"You weren't here when Mother died," he said.

"For God's sake, Ernst, get a hold of yourself. I was in the army. It was the war. I had just been in Caporetto. I had no control over where I was. It was yes-sir, no-sir, shoot-at-that-Italian-over-there, sir. I was in the damn war."

"You weren't here when she died. You didn't have to watch it. Actually, we couldn't watch it, either. She got sick one day and was dead two days later — and we weren't even allowed to be near her the last day."

Ernst wiped away a tear.

"And you weren't here," he said.

Back in the chair again. Another tear, another quick flick with his finger. Another measure poured into the glass. None for me.

"You weren't here to do the work," Ernst said. "You could never do the work. It's a business, after all. It's getting up and putting on a suit and putting your ass in that chair over there."

Pause. Point at the desk.

"It's dealing with the old man's bullshit," he said. "It's hiring and firing and getting the machinery fixed when it breaks down. It's all of the messy stuff, all of the hard stuff. You and Otto — you always drank from the tit, and drank fucking well, but you never dealt with anything you didn't want to deal with."

"That's not fair," I said.

"The hell it isn't."

"The old man hated me."

"That's complete bullshit."

"He fucking snarled at me."

"He didn't hate you," Ernst said. "He was disappointed in you. There's a big difference."

The last bit, the "he was disappointed in you," was delivered barely above a whisper. And it stung. It hit me in a way that I couldn't remember being hit before. *He was disappointed in you.* Jesus.

In my heart, I guess I had always known this to be the truth — although he did fucking hate me, too. He never supported me, not before I left and not after. That also was the truth, and I wasn't going to be made to feel guilty by my brother because I had chosen the better life.

"Nobody forced you to fucking stay," I said.

"Now who's lying?"

"You could have gone."

"You were 16 when you left," he said. "I was 14. There was no way I could get away."

"You didn't want to get away. You fucking lusted after that seat at the big goddamned desk."

"I was 14."

"It's what you wanted. It's not my fault it didn't turn out the way you hoped."

"It could have turned out different for me if you had stayed," Ernst said. "I could have been the one to find a happier path."

"You don't know what happy is — never did, never will," I said.

"Thanks to you."

"So, your life is my fault? Is that how you really see it?

Because if it is, I don't know. I can't think of anything more pathetic than that."

"It's the truth."

"Bullshit."

"And I guess the truth hurts, you fucking disappointment," Ernst said. "Because that's what the old man always said. He'd look at Otto's expenses and just say, 'What a fucking thief.' And then he'd look at yours, really look at them, and shake his head and say — really, just above a whisper — 'What a fucking disappointment.'"

And that's pretty much where it ended. Rather than scream back at him anymore, I finished my drink and took a deep breath. Then I stood up and began to walk toward the door.

"See you in 30 years," I said.

"See you in hell," my brother said.

19

The walk up to Petrin Tower was brutal. No other word for it. You walked over the Charles Bridge and through the part of town that was on the other side. At the beginning, it was a gentle upslope. After a certain point, though, it was straight uphill. Brutal.

Along the way — maybe halfway up, give or take — there was the entrance to a small park on the right, a small park with a couple of small benches. And, well, let's just say that those benches were screaming my name.

"You doing all right, old man?" Maria said.

"I'd tell you go to fuck yourself if I knew you better," I said.

We sat on the benches for a few minutes and began talking. Within a few seconds, she was bitching about her family and I was bitching about my brother.

The truth was, I had managed to purge myself of most of the anger and bitterness by the time the train from Brno had returned to Prague. God bless those flimsy papers cups. The way I had figured it, Ernst had been an asshole when we were kids, and I had believed he was an asshole for the last 30 years, and now I had a final bit of confirmation. I had been the bigger man, and I had made the effort, and I had been rebuffed. I had lost nothing but the train fare, and I had gained the certainty that my instincts had always been right, and that an asshole doesn't change his spots, or some such thing.

Still, I guess I hadn't jettisoned the whole thing completely, in that I felt the need to retell the whole story to Maria.

"Sounds like a pathetic jerk, your brother, maybe more pathetic than jerk," she said, after I was done. But then she changed the subject immediately, changed it to her family, to her sister, "the goddamned dreamer."

"You don't dream?" I said.

"I'm rooted in reality. In this country, you have to be. In the last dozen years, we've gone from being run by limp-dicked dreamers, to Nazis, to Communists. You live through that and you don't tend to spend a lot of time with your head in the clouds."

After a few more minutes on the bench, we got going again. The hills were unrelenting, and that was bad enough. Then came the steps — a hundred or so, in groups of a dozen with a landing in between. Then a pause, and then another hundred or so. Christ.

"You know, there is a funicular," she said.

"Now you tell me."

"This is the native experience."

"I'm not a native."

"And not a kid anymore."

"Again, if I knew you a little better—"

"Fuck myself," Maria said. "Got it."

We finally reached the top of the last staircase, and I needed another minute on a bench. Then we walked through some trees, and the Petrin Tower was off to our left. It was, uh, unimpressive, and I guess my face suggested as much, and Maria looked at me with a pout and said, "What?"

"You said it was as big as the Eiffel Tower. It isn't close."

"You've been?"

I nodded. I didn't feel the need to enlighten her about my years during the war, my years in the French Resistance. I might have hinted at it — I wasn't sure, which wasn't a good thing for a spy — but I wasn't positive. Whatever. She accepted the nod and moved on.

"I didn't say it was as big as the Eiffel Tower," she said.

"You said it was as tall."

"That's not what I said. The truth is, as they taught us in school, Petrin Tower was built on a 1-to-5 scale compared to the Eiffel Tower. But what I said was, it's as high — and it is. When you get to the top, and measure the elevation above sea level, it's the same as the elevation at the top of the Eiffel Tower."

"A bit of false advertising from you," I said.

"A bit hard of hearing from you," Maria said.

The walk to the top of the tower was another 300 steps, "give or take," she said. I really did think I might have a heart attack by the time we reached the top.

"Worth it, though?" she said, with a wave of her arm at the panorama of the view.

"Yeah, nice," I said. It had taken me a few seconds, but I had managed to stop gulping for air. I was still sweating though, and needed to mop my forehead with my sleeve.

"Nice? That's the best you can do? Nice? You're such a romantic."

"Very nice, then," I said.

We walked around the narrow platform at the top and took in the view from every angle. Rooftops, then forests, then... whatever. There wasn't a holy-shit view of anything, at least not from my vantage point. About halfway around, Maria stopped and pointed.

"That's west," she said.

I nodded. It hit me that I was doing a lot of nodding.

"My sister swore that she could see West Germany from here."

"How far is it?"

"A hundred miles, give or take."

"I don't know."

"She swore, and she said it's science."

"Since when is philosophy a science?"

"That's exactly what I told her," Maria said.

We stayed up on the viewing level for about 15 minutes, drinking it all in. Okay, very nice. We were sharing the view with a group of teenagers and somebody who looked like one of their teachers. The kids were all horsing around and the teacher was leaning against a post, eyes closed, likely steeling himself for what was probably to come. That is, an upcoming lunch at the little restaurant near the base of the tower, a lunch where the boys would begin wadding up paper napkins and firing them at each other. That likely would happen before the menus even arrived.

We eventually left the teenagers and began walking back down. At one of the landings built into the spiral staircase, we stopped and kissed. When I thought back on it later, the whole thing seemed natural enough, but there was no doubt in my mind that Maria had been the aggressor. We hadn't so much as held hands by that point, but there she was, leaning in. I remembered that clearly, and I also remembered that we almost got knocked off of our feet, not by the kiss but by a gust of wind that had been funneled through an opening in the metal structure of the tower.

We continued our embrace as we shuffled our feet and stabilized ourselves. I made a crack about her kissing superpowers and then Maria reached down and made a digital inspection of what was down there, down below my belt. Her hand lingered, gently, for several seconds.

"OK, not dead yet," she said.

We walked down the rest of the steps of the tower, and down the hill, and directly to an apartment that was not Maria's. She produced a key and said, "A friend's. For, you know."

"I think I know."

"I hope you know."

We were getting undressed in rather a hurry, kissing and not talking much. But there was one conversation Maria insisted on having as the bits of clothing flew about.

"You didn't with her, right?" she said.

Her. Her sister, Lidia. Back in the displaced persons camp in Ravensburg.

"No, no," I lied. "We had a quick bond but it was platonic, at least on my end."

"This better not be something you're doing so that you can tell your buddies that you banged two sisters."

"No, of course not. No friends to tell, even if it did happen — which it didn't."

We slept together, and then we slept together again a half-hour later. Maria's only comment was, "Not bad, old man. Not bad."

I lay back silently, and decided against the reflexive "fuck you," and just accepted the compliment. And then I closed my eyes and, well, I couldn't help but think about the story I would have to tell the next time I saw Leon.

20

Finally, on the 10th day, Vilem made contact. The procedure would be the same as before, but without the passwords. Another train trip to the ass end of Karlsbad. Another series of loops around the train station until his car pulled up along the curb. Another trip out to the woods, and then to the little road, and then to the clearing with the two facing tree stumps. Another festival of chain smoking and farting.

"You ever think about changing your diet? I mean, fuck," I said.

"Not my diet. My nerves."

"Well, calm the hell down, then. Have a drink. Do something. You're going to asphyxiate me before I can get you out."

After we got to our respective tree stumps, I pulled out my little penlight and my notebook.

"Shoot," I said.

"But I have something I want to say."

"Give me what I need, and then I'll listen."

Working from memory, Vilem supplied me with more names of Czech agents working in West Germany and more information on the names he had already given me. It really was a pretty neat party trick, his ability to rattle off names and addresses and identifying characteristics — the two most memorable were "short blonde hair, small tits" and "big fucking mole, right cheek" — without the assistance of any notes. I would easily be able to fill another page with secret writing when I got back.

I'd had to tell him to slow down more than once as he spat information at me, and I scribbled in my notebook. After his last burst, it probably took me 15 seconds to get it all down.

"That it?" I said.

"That's fucking plenty, more than your money's worth."

"I didn't say it wasn't."

"Your tone…"

"No tone," I said. "Don't be so sensitive."

"How can I not be sensitive? I'm betraying my country, and if they ever find out, they'll string me up by my balls."

"They won't find out."

"Says you,"

"I promise."

"Fuck your promises," Vilem said. "When are you getting me out?"

"Two weeks."

"No, no. Two weeks? That's too long."

"We can hide you."

"Too long."

"Best I can do," I said, and that really was the truth. Arranging for the transportation was apparently the biggest issue. Skippy and his people didn't have a car. They were going to have to steal one and find new license plates, and it seems they weren't entirely equipped for the endeavor. Then, I was insisting on them being able to identify at least a hint of a safe place to cross the border — not necessarily with the car, just anywhere. They had put out the word to their people in the hinterlands — "two old fucks with a goat," Skippy had said, with too much cynicism for a kid — and were waiting for a reply. He probably wasn't wrong, except for maybe the part about the goat. It might have been a cow.

"Where can you hide me?" Vilem said.

"Prague. It's a big city."

"I don't know."

"You don't know if it's a big city?"

Vilem stood up, walked away, let loose.

"I don't know," he said. "And besides, there's something else I need."

The wife. I had figured as much. She was in her thirties, like him, and as long as she didn't normally require a wheelbarrow to transport her around Karlsbad, I guessed that we were fine. Two of us or three of us — it didn't really matter. One person was the simplest, obviously. If it was just me, that would be a cinch. Adding the second person, Vilem, was a complication. But adding the wife, going from two people to three, really wouldn't be an additional issue as long as we could fit in the car and as long as she didn't insist on bringing her entire wardrobe with her.

"She can only bring one bag that she can carry herself," I said.

"What are you talking about?"

"Your wife."

"What about my wife?"

"You're about to ask me to get her out, too."

"The fuck I am," Vilem said.

Interesting.

"Girlfriend?" I said.

"Not her, either," he said.

A wife and a girlfriend. Young Vilem really was an expert at keeping secrets.

"So if it's not that, what do you need?" I said. "Not more money. We already agreed, and if you think you're going to fucking play me and try to shake me down now—"

"Relax, it's not money. The money is fine. I need to get somebody else out, though. You were right about that."

"Okay, who?"

At which point, Vilem launched into a story about his best friend growing up. Karl. Inseparable as kids, they were conscripted at the end of war, dragged into the same unit of a kind of home guard in Prague, but they never saw any meaningful action. It was after the war, though, after the Communists arrived and never left, that Vilem drifted into the intelligence business and Karl veered into the dissident writer business. They didn't stay close — couldn't stay close — but they managed to have a single annual all-day drunk at a bar in the old neighborhood. October 17th, every year, and he said they never missed.

"It's funny," Vilem said. "But every year, around the fifth or sixth beer, we have the same conversation. I tell him that I'm still not sure how I ended up doing what I did, and he tells me he's still not sure how he ended up where he was. It's funny. I tell him I'm just like a clerk, and he tells me that he's not much of a zealot but somebody who just plays the part of a zealot, like an actor. But he says it's all he knows at this point, and I say it's all I know — and then we just shake our heads and tell stories about when we were 12."

Six months ago, Vilem said, the people in charge of such things had had enough of Karl's anti-Communist writings. They scooped him up and tossed him into what they referred to as a "re-education camp." And that's where Karl had been ever since.

"And you know what they have him doing?" Vilem said. "Building that massive fucking Stalin statue."

"Where?"

"Along the river. You've never seen it?"

"What, that giant thing—"

"Is a statue of that giant asshole," he said. "Going to be, anyway. Been building it for months. Not close to finished."

I thought for a second and realized that this was a real complication. The wife or the girlfriend would have been a hell of a lot easier.

"How am I supposed to break somebody out of a labor camp?" I said. "I don't know shit about any of that. I mean, the risk — to me, to you — would be..."

"No, no, no," Vilem said. "You don't have to break him out. I can handle all of that. I mean, it's not like it's a prison. They sleep in tents. They're not shackled to the ground. There's no bars on the doors. I mean, there's no fucking doors. And you're permitted to leave occasionally to see your family."

"And they come back?"

"They come back if they don't want their family to be touched. But the only family Karl has left is his father, who has cancer. The old man doesn't have three months left. The two of them have talked about it. I can get the paperwork to get Karl released for a day — it'll all be legitimate, real paperwork, and it won't be questioned. Not initially, anyway. But the paperwork will get Karl out, and he'll leave his father and make a run for it with me. They won't touch a dying man. I mean, even they wouldn't do that."

"He's not sick or anything, right?" I said.

"Didn't you hear me — he's dying."

"Not the father. I mean Karl."

"What about him?"

"He can move okay, right? Like, they've been feeding him for the last six months and everything? Because we can't begin to—"

"He's fine," Vilem said. "He's more than fine. The truth is, he's as fit as a goddamned fiddle. Christ, he lifts boulders and mixes cement all day. He could fucking carry you if it came to that."

I asked a few more questions about the logistics, and Vilem seemed to have thought it through. All of the contingencies I could come up with were covered. All Vilem needed was the date, and I told him I would have to get back to him.

He drove me back to the station in Karlsbad and dropped me a few blocks away.

"You sure about your wife?" I said.

"Completely," he said.

"We can't handle last-minute changes."

"I'm completely sure," Vilem said.

21

Jan was wiping down the bar at The Eagles when I got back from Karlsbad.

"Pretty late," I said.

"Couldn't sleep," he said.

"Something on your mind?"

"Something like that."

"I'll listen if you want."

"Fuck it," Jan said, grabbing a bottle and two glasses.

We each drank a measure of whatever he had poured — some kind of whisky — and didn't say anything. He refilled the glasses and looked at me, and I half arched an eyebrow.

"They were here today," he said.

"Who was here today?"

"They. The big they. The they with a capital T."

The secret police.

"Czech or Russian?" I said.

"One of each."

"Is that normal?"

"It is very much not normal," Jan said. "I mean, the questions were the same as always."

"Meaning?

"'How's business? Have you had anyone stay over in your apartment? Anybody new or is it mostly regulars? Do you ever overhear anything that might interest us?' Shit like that. I get those monthly, so it's not like the questions themselves were the problem. It was the Russian being there. I'm used to the Czech bastards. I don't know. Maybe it's nothing. But I've been pissing double all night."

We drank. I didn't know what to say.

"Oh yeah, I forgot. They wanted to see upstairs. That hasn't happened except for the first time, when they were doing their first census of available rooms. Hell, two years ago, probably. Thank God you put the bed away — I check every day, by the way. You're a star tenant. It just looked like a messy storeroom, like always. Like it's supposed to be. Thank God."

We had a third drink, and I tried to calm him down. The truth was, though, that I was more worried than Jan. For all I knew, they had somebody watching the door now — except that it was a tiny street, almost more an alley than a street, and there wasn't an obvious place for a watcher to hide. That we had been drinking for a half-hour — well after closing time — and nobody in a black trench coat had burst through the door told me that I could relax. But, still. I really was worried.

Up in the storeroom that night, my hand was shaking a little bit as I started writing out the new message with the secret chemical carbon paper. I settled down quickly enough, but this visit from the Czech-Soviet tag team wasn't nothing. Maybe it wasn't everything but it wasn't nothing, either.

Two more weeks. That's all I kept thinking about. Two more weeks until they could steal a car, and get a clean license plate, and map at least an approximate route over the border and into West Germany. Two weeks. I had to get a hold of Skippy and push him. Two weeks. There wasn't enough alcohol in Prague to get me through that long in one piece.

I was afraid to carry the letter in my pocket when I walked to the bench along the river — so I cut the smallest opening into the hem of the lining of my coat, just a couple of stitches, and shoved the twice-folded letter into the hole. It was a half-assed bit of concealing it, but I didn't know what else to do. I mean, half-assed was better than bare-assed.

As it turned out, I didn't see a soul during my walk. Under a street lamp, I checked my wristwatch. 5:12 a.m. The hours of the job were going to kill me before a bullet did — I was convinced of that, more convinced with each passing year. I actually laughed at the thought before I remembered Jan's Czech-Soviet tag team. It was a nice interlude, the laugh. It didn't last a second but it was lovely.

I fished the letter out of my coat's lining, taped it to the underside of the bench, and felt better. A little better, anyway. You turn a big job into small tasks and then you tick them off, one by one. There was pleasure in the tick marks, even if they were mental.

That bit of satisfaction lasted longer than the laugh — between five and 10 minutes. That's when I got back to Old Town Square, and looked at the big black statue, and saw three new X's chalked into place.

XXX. An emergency meeting. Fuck me.

I looked at my watch: 5:40. God, I needed some sleep. But the rules of an emergency meeting signal were that I was to go back to the St. Norbert statue on the bridge at the next multiple of six. So, 6 a.m., or noon, or 6 p.m., or midnight — and my contact would be there. Marek, Skippy the Spy — I promised myself that I would fucking brain him if this really wasn't an emergency. But then I thought about Jan and his visitors. And I wondered about Vilem and his army overlords. And I thought about two weeks. And I looked at my watch again: 5:41. And I started walking in the direction of the Charles Bridge.

I didn't hesitate at all as I approached because, as it turned out, there were plenty of people on the bridge at that time of day — mostly older people, the kind that had lost the ability to sleep in. Couples strolling. Dogs being walked. A vendor of some sort slowly pushing a big wooden cart. Old men smoking and leaning over the railing. It wasn't packed but nobody who wasn't looking for me would see me as anything other than a part of the passing parade.

As I neared the St. Norbert statue, Marek was standing right next to it, hands in his pockets. The breeze off of the water did chill the whole place.

"Skippy, this better be fucking good," I said.

"What did you call me?"

I ignored him.

"Well?" I said.

He pointed me toward the railing that faced south. A man was leaning against it, a man wearing a coat and a hat like a dozen others I had walked past as I crossed over from the old town side of the bridge. He didn't see me as I walked over and didn't appear to hear my footsteps as I approached.

And he only half turned when he said, "It's about fucking time."

And then he turned all the way and faced me.

It was Fritz.

22

"We should go."

It was Marek, from over my shoulder. I had hugged Fritz but hadn't received an explanation.

"Do you see something? Someone?" Fritz said. He was speaking to Marek, not me.

"No, but... we should just go," he said. Fritz and Skippy, planning my life. Christ.

The three of us walked away from the old town side of the bridge and into the neighborhood on the other side. The uphill had already begun, and all I could think about was walking up to Petrin Tower with Maria. But we turned left quickly enough and walked into a bar on the corner. I didn't see the name.

At a quarter after 6 in the morning, the place was doing significant business. More than half of the barstools were taken and more than half of the tables, too.

I looked at Skippy with a question on my face, and he said, "They work third shift at the box factory."

He pointed toward the back of the bar.

"It's about two blocks that way," he said. "They get off at 6. They're here by 6:05."

"A box factory runs three shifts a day?" I said.

"It's a worker's paradise," Skippy said.

"Wiseass," I said.

He grinned. Fritz had already ordered three beers, and they had been placed in front of him. He handed them out and said, "Marek, you've done well with the whole thing. This is perfect. But the conversation from here on is for Alex's ears only. I need you to stay here at the bar and watch the door, just in case. Alex and I are to sit at that last table in the back."

Skippy nodded as solemnly as he could, but the attaboy from Fritz had hit home. You could see the happiness in his eyes. We left him there at the bar and grabbed the table along the back wall.

"He's good, right?" Fritz said.

"He's a kid."

"But he's a good kid, right?"

I shrugged.

"So, he's very good, right?"

"This is no life for a kid."

"You're not his father."

"He's very young."

"We all have to grow up sometime," Fritz said. "Except maybe you."

I asked him about his travels and he waved me off.

"The papers are a pretty good forgery, and I'm an old man, and nobody gives old people a second look," he said. "It's really a benefit. Old ladies are even better — it's like they're invisible."

I shrugged again, and we drank.

"Your army captain is a goldmine," he said.

"And there's more — I just left the next envelope at the dead drop. Do they go straight to you — because if they do, we could just go scoop it up now."

"No, not to me. It goes to headquarters in Pullach. I get the information after they get done doing whatever they do to it. It's a quick turnaround — they have the stuff for about a day and then they courier it to me in Vienna. But there's more?"

"A lot more — names, other shit."

"It's a shame he won't stay in place."

"I know, but…"

"Yeah. It's still a great victory for us," he said.

Fritz's glass was empty. He looked down at it, seeming to study the lace of foam on the sides.

"So, what the hell is this about?" I said.

"It's complicated. But there's something I need to tell you."

"I gathered as much. But you couldn't just send a message?"

"No, this one needed to be in person," Fritz said.

He took a breath, then another.

"You know about the show trials?" he said.

"Yeah, I went to one."

"You what?"

"I wandered into one," I said. "And it was a full goddamned show, let me tell you. The poor fucker on the witness stand, it was like he was brainwashed or something. He ended up confessing to everything except shooting the archduke. And the crowd around me was more than entertained. It was some sick shit. Diabolical. Twisted."

Fritz nodded. Another deep breath.

"We have a guy kind of high up in the government bureaucracy," he said. "Not real high, but high enough. He traffic-cops a lot of the paperwork between the Justice Ministry and the propaganda people."

"Justice Ministry," I said. "Interesting name, that."

"Yeah, yeah. Ironic. Anyway, he sees stuff that can sometimes be helpful. Not earth-shattering, but helpful. Gives you some context, some texture. You know what I mean?"

"I guess."

"So, here's the thing," Fritz said. "We just got a packet from our guy — two days ago, I think. Yeah, two days. It's been hectic since then."

"And?"

"There's going to be a new series of show trials, and they're likely to begin in the coming weeks. You're right. They sense that the public has been eating them up, and it's been their most effective way to simultaneously entertain the average man on the street and also scare the hell out of him."

"A real twofer, that."

"Exactly," Fritz said. "Anyway, five trials coming up in the next few weeks, probably. Based on the paperwork, the arrests are said to be imminent. Well, six, seven days, something like that. They like to make it look legal, so they do have to file actual arrest warrants and run them by the higher-ups in the Justice Ministry before the process stars. From what our guy said, the warrants will be approved and the arrests made in a couple of days. Six, seven days. Very soon, very—"

A loud crash and then some shouting stopped Fritz in mid-sentence. We both turned to the bar. It was Skippy, and he was in the middle of a fight with the guy on the adjacent barstool. He was whaling away, our Skippy, battering the poor guy next to him. It was bad enough that most of the rest of the bar was now on its feet and joining in to assist their mate from the box factory. Skippy was going to get clobbered.

I stood up, reflexively.

Fritz grabbed me.

"Wait," he said. "Look."

At the end of the bar that was nearest to the front door, there were two black trench coats. One of them was holding what looked to be a guy's papers in his hand and was studying them with the aid of a little penlight.

"Come on," Fritz said. The entire bar was on its feet, and two guys were now taking turns on Skippy with balled fists. At least nobody had picked up a chair. Fritz walked toward the single doorway along the back wall. It led to the toilets, which were down a narrow hallway. At the end of the hallway, there was another door that ended up dumping us into a back alley. You could feel the chill in the darkness.

"You think he—"

"Of course he did," Fritz said. "The kid is good."

"I hope the kid isn't dead."

"Nah," Fritz said. "I have to figure, for the regular clientele, a little fisticuffs is just part of the weekly entertainment. They'll just throw him out on his ass. The secret police might look at his papers, but it won't be anything. They're not in the business of breaking up bar fights. Small risk for him overall — and for all we know, he might end up running out of the same back door in a minute."

"You think the trench coats—"

"Were for us?" Fritz said. "Hard to know for sure. Have you had any, you know, incidents? Hints of trouble?"

We had exited the alley by then. The morning had gotten brighter in just the 15 minutes we had been in the bar, and I squinted for a second as we emerged from the alley's shadows. Fritz wanted to walk left but I shook my head.

"It's straight fucking uphill that way," I said. "I've done it. You've got to believe me — it was hard for me. It'll be brutal for you."

"I'm fine."

"Trust me. Back to the bridge is the best. I know the other side a lot better than I know this side. It'll be even busier now than it was — and it's downhill. Really, trust me."

While we walked, I told him about the Czech-Soviet tag team that had visited The Eagle, and how it did spook me a bit. Fritz took it all in as we walked. He shrugged.

"It was a quick glance, but it looked like they were just in to check a few sets of papers," he said. "Can't be sure, but it seemed routine. Either way, Marek did the smart thing, creating the diversion."

I nodded. Fucking Skippy.

We were back on the Charles Bridge, halfway over. It was, indeed, even busier than it had been earlier. I couldn't be positive, but I was pretty sure that we weren't being followed or even noticed by anyone.

"So, the arrests?" I said.

"Yeah."

"I mean, am I on the list somehow? That doesn't make any sense — like, none. None at all. How could they even know my name?"

"No," Fritz said. "It's not you."

He stopped walking. I stopped walking after half bumping into him. He turned to face me and put a hand on each of my shoulders.

And then, Fritz said, "But the five arrest warrants, well, one of them is for your brother."

PART III

23

"**B**ut I really want to stay," Alex said.

"You don't know what you really want," said Otto, his uncle. "You're 16 years old. We're in the middle of a goddamned war about who-knows-what. The world is upside down, and you don't know what you want."

"I do. I want Vienna."

"You're thinking with your dick."

"What does that mean?"

"Don't kid a kidder," Otto said. "I mean, don't even try. All the girls here, so many more than in Brno — come on. I've seen you. Don't even try."

"It's not that," Alex said.

"Your smile says otherwise."

"It's not that. And you know it's not that. You tell me not to kid a kidder. Well, I'm saying the same thing back to you. You know what I'm saying. You know me. Fuck, you were me back in the day."

"Fuck, is it?"

"An adult conversation between adults," Alex said.

They were sitting in a café on the Karntnerstrasse. There was a war going on, sure, but it had not touched Vienna. Food was still plen-

tiful, goods available. It was a Sunday and it looked like every Sunday when the weather was nice. People dressed for church, walking home from the Stephansdom, window shopping. Packs of girls and boys in their teens and twenties, eyeing up each other. Otto and Alex each sipped a beer. The fun uncle. "But just one."

The sun was in Otto's eyes. He adjusted the angle of his chair and faced Alex just a bit more directly.

"I wasn't you, I was older," he said.

"How much older?"

"Four years. A big difference, those four years. A lot happens to a boy in those four years."

"I have had sex, you know," Alex said.

Otto made a face. A questioning face.

"Well, with our hands," Alex said.

"Quite an adult conversation."

Otto took a sip and took the measure of his nephew. It had been less than a month, but Otto had clearly seen it. He knew what the kid was saying was correct. They were the same. Goddammit.

"You were older, but it will be easier for me," Alex said. "You came here by yourself. You opened the office by yourself. You went to the meetings with the clients by yourself. Did you have to find the clients?"

"No, a group of them were already established," Otto said. "I added new clients — I almost doubled the number over the years. But the initial list, those contacts were all by mail, for the most part. Some telephone in an emergency — not everybody had one back then — but mostly by mail or wire. It really wasn't a satisfactory arrangement for either side. The clients wanted more hand-holding and my father wanted more personal selling to get them to up their orders. I came up with the idea of being the rep in Austria and Germany. That's why my father agreed in the end — because it was a damn good idea and it made him money."

"I can make money," Alex said. He had gotten quieter.

"It's not the same."

"You can teach me."

"It's not the same," Otto said.

They both sipped and watched the passing parade. Both of them were distracted by a crying child begging for an ice cream — screaming, picked up by her father, tugging at the man's nose and just wailing. After about five seconds, the toddler won.

"You know I can help you," Alex said. "I've heard you say two or three times that you've got too much on your plate. I could take some of the shit clients off of your hands."

"No such thing as a shit client. First rule."

"The smaller clients. You could teach me, and then you could concentrate on the big contracts. You know, you're not getting any younger."

"Easy there."

"Truth is truth in an adult conversation," Alex said.

Otto sipped. He didn't hate the idea. The truth was, he had already gamed it out in his head. Alex would need to finish school, but he could show him the ropes and take him on a trip or two to show him how the whole thing was done. He didn't know a lot about the after-meetings part of the job — Alex thought it was wining and dining, not carousing and sometimes pimping — and he would have to be enlightened on the subject. He'd have to be 18 before he could really be of any help, and that would only be if Alex was a quick study.

But he would be a quick study — Otto sensed that almost immediately. They really were the same person.

"I can't go back to him," Alex said. Him. Alex's father, Otto's younger brother.

"Why not?"

"You know why not — and besides, he doesn't need me. He has Ernst. Christ, they're already attached at the hip. Do you know, my

father dresses him up in a goddamn business suit and takes him to work sometimes?"

"Twice a month," Otto said, half in a whisper.

"Yeah, twice a month. How did you know?"

"Because that's how often my father took your father into the office at that age. Got permission from the headmaster and everything."

Stop. Sip.

"Joined at the hip," Otto said.

The thing that scared Otto the most was that, if Alex stayed, he would be responsible for him. Otto had been responsible for nothing except himself and he liked it that way. Adding a teenage boy into his world would change it, he knew, but would it tilt that world so wildly off of its axis that Otto couldn't recognize it anymore?

That was the worry. But there was the flip side, too. Part of him wanted a family connection again. And part of him wanted the chance to influence someone, to shape their life — a better life, he knew, than sitting across from his father in Brno at that giant partner's desk.

"I was a little bit older than you, maybe 18," Otto said. "The old man, he took the family to dinner — it was some occasion, I forget. We went to Miller's, which was the best restaurant in Brno at the time. At least, I thought it was the best — but I was only a kid, so who the hell knew?"

Alex was leaning forward, both elbows on the little café table.

"My old man, your grandfather, he was so conservative, so uptight, I wondered sometimes if he was even able to have a good shit. And cheap, too. Painfully cheap.

"So, we're at Miller's, and it's all white table cloths and snooty waiters. They hand out the menus, and we all peruse, but I knew what I wanted. The waiter came to me, and I said, 'I'll have a steak, medium rare.' My father didn't say anything, but he made a face and shook his head. I mean, I was used to it. The old man, old Jacob Kovacs — I called him Jake the Snake when I was talking to your

father about him — well, that was his standard reply to pretty much everything I ever said or did. But it just hit me harder that time, for some reason. And so, I announced loudly enough for the whole restaurant to hear, 'Austerity should be a temporary condition, not a way of life!'"

Alex's eyes were wide.

"So, you really do understand, deep down," he said.

"Deep down," Otto said.

Pause, sip.

"To this day, it's the best steak I've ever had."

Pause, sip. Wave to the waiter.

"Two more," Uncle Otto said.

24

————

I hustled Fritz into a small café where I'd had breakfast the previous week, hustled him while trying to simultaneously convince my heart not to explode inside my chest. Ernst. Jesus.

It was a no frills place. Coffee and a hard-boiled egg for each of us. We were at the back corner table, with a view of the front door, just in case. We didn't talk until the food had been delivered.

"It's all I know," Fritz said. "Well, I know the general charge — 'theft from the people' — but that's what they charge everybody with in these things. It's some kind of financial shenanigans. But that's it. He's on the list, Ernst Kovacs of Brno. That's really all I've got."

For a second, I drifted to the show trial I had attended. The poor bastard on the witness stand had likely chiseled a bit on the margins, something that a lot of people figure is just aggressive capitalism. But from those margins, the government responded with a two-by-four between the eyes. Ernst? Who knew?

"You know, I went to see him the other day," I said.

"Whoa. First time in..."

"In forever."

"And how did it go?"

"Badly enough that I wished I hadn't gone," I said. "But, well, that's really true. He was a complete dick, and he blamed me for his pathetic life and for the fact that first the Nazis took the mine away from the family and now the Commies were about to do the same thing. But I guess I'm glad I went. Proved I'm the bigger man, or some such shit."

Fritz peeled the shell off of the egg. His hands were shaking — not a ton, but some. The operation took twice as long as it should have. He was in his mid-seventies, after all.

"You're as good a man as I know," he said.

I banged on the side of my head as if I was knocking some water out of my ear after a swim.

"I'm not sure I heard what you said."

"Fuck you — did you hear that?" Fritz said.

"Loud and clear," I said. The whole thing. I actually was touched. Fritz and I had grown closer over the decades. He had started as somebody who tended to use me for his purposes and then protect me from the fallout. But over time, while it was an employer-employee relationship, it had become something more than that. Otto had been dead for close to 15 years, and if Fritz had tried to replace his good friend as a kind of surrogate uncle to me, I don't know. It wasn't quite that, but it was nudging in that direction.

I told him a little bit about the house and about the mine, and that Willy the caretaker was still there and showed me my parents' graves down by the river bank.

"How long's the old man been dead?"

"Six, seven years. Heart attack. Ernst said it was because he bottled up the rage about the Nazis taking the mine. He sort of said that it was my fault, too, for not giving back the sliver of my rightful inheritance that he'd paid me to get rid of me."

"Good God."

"Exactly," I said. "Old home week."

"You going to eat that?" Fritz said. He pointed at my untouched egg, and I shook my head. He unpeeled the second one much quicker than the first.

With his mouth half full, Fritz said, "We can handle this any way you want."

"What do you mean?"

"Are you inclined to help your brother or not?"

"To be honest? I'm not sure," I said.

That was the truth, too. I didn't know what I wanted to do and I didn't know what was exactly possible. I already had Vilem and his childhood pal in the labor camp, and that seemed to me to be a pretty full plate. Where Ernst might fit was, well, I just had no idea. And whether I wanted him to fit, after everything, I had even less of an idea about that.

"If the answer is no, then we ignore it," Fritz said. "But, like I said, if you do want to help him, we can help you. We can play this a couple of different ways — at least, that's what I came up with on the train."

"Okay, lay it out for me. My mind's racing. Like, I can't focus. I can't fucking think straight about any of this."

"Perfectly understandable," he said. "Perfectly, completely. So, listen to Uncle Fritz here. If you want to drop your army captain and his buddy, we'll get somebody else to take care of them and get them over the border. Hell, I might do it myself."

"The fuck you will," I said.

"It's not that far-fetched. I told you how old people are invisible. I could make it work for me."

"I repeat: the fuck you will. If that's the option, forget it. And Skippy can't be the option, either."

"Skippy?"

"Marek. He's too young, and I won't even have half a discussion about that. Not you, not him."

Fritz stated laughing, a little soft laugh. Then he said, "Skippy. You are a real asshole."

The waiter came by and offered more coffee. We accepted. It took a minute because it always takes a minute. In American movies in the things they call diners, the waitress just walks around with a pot of coffee and refills you on the spot. A much better system.

"So, what's your Plan B?" I said.

"Just add Ernst to the current package," he said. "We'll adjust the transportation accordingly, make sure it's a big enough car. We'll be extra careful about finding you a proper route to the border. We'll arrange a distraction of sorts, if it makes sense. A traitor, a Commie sympathizer, an asshole brother, and you. The Good Shepherd, that's you. You could write a book about it when you're done."

"At least a chapter," I said.

We drank the second cup of coffee and then a third. Fritz didn't say much and I really didn't either, other than the occasional stream-of-consciousness rambling about how this might all get pulled together and how Ernst might screw it all up.

As we both stared into the dregs of our cups, Fritz said, "You know, I have to get out of here. My transport leaves in," he looked at his watch, "two hours."

"Yeah, yeah," I said.

We walked outside. The morning had clouded over.

"So?" he said.

"Here's what I think I want to do," I said. "I'll go to Brno, tell him, try to gauge his reaction. If he just kicks me out, fine. Clear conscience and ready to go with the other two. If he wants my help, well, okay. Then I handle it from there, seat of my pants, me and the three goddamned musketeers. The car will be fine either way, I'm sure, and they're either going to get us a good route to the border or they aren't. It really doesn't change if Ernst comes or not. And the rest of the details, well, are you willing to trust me with that?"

"So you've really decided to make the offer to bring him out?"

I nodded.

Fritz whistled and shook his head.

"Of course I'm going to make the offer, old man," I said. "Don't forget, I'm the best guy you know."

"Not the best — as good a man as I know," he said.

"Same difference," I said. And I actually gave him a hug on the street before he walked away.

25

Later on the same afternoon, it was time to spring Vilem's childhood friend from the labor camp. The way we had worked it out, Vilem would take the train in from Karlsbad and, this time, it would be me waiting for him in the car. In this case, it was the car that belonged to Skippy's father.

"He loan it to you often?" I said.

"Enough."

"You ever feel up a girl in the back seat?"

"You that hard up for a jerk-off fantasy?" he said. Again with the grin.

I left him on the street corner and drove toward the station. The train was late, and I was parked at the curb for nearly a half-hour before Vilem emerged. He was in full uniform, and I looked him up and down as he got in the passenger seat.

"Really? The whole shebang?" I said.

"Official business. Full uniform," he said.

I tried to approach the construction site directly, but Vilem told me to make a turn I didn't expect, a turn seemingly away from where we should be headed.

"Trust me, it's faster," he said. "We kind of come at it from behind this way and miss all the traffic."

We ended up driving through some parkland and then, as he said, approaching the construction site from behind. Off to the left, about 100 yards away, were three large tents.

"Karl's humble abode for the last few months," Vilem said, pointing. "But we're headed the other way to start."

Nearer to where the statue was being worked on, there was a small wooden building that was actually an overgrown shack. I'd hate to have been inside during a storm. Inside were two corporals and one officer. Vilem took us to the officer, pulled some paperwork from his pocket, and handed it over.

"His father?" the officer said. Captain, I thought.

"Cancer. Not much time," Vilem said. "We grew up in the same neighborhood. My mother called."

The captain nodded. He began to stick out his hand and, without asking, Vilem handed him his military identification.

The captain nodded again, handed the identification back, and kept reading. From where I was standing, I could see that Vilem's name was at the bottom of the paper along with what appeared to be his signature.

"And with you here is who?"

"A cousin. Taking them together, just a courtesy."

The captain looked at me for several seconds and then said, "My condolences."

I nodded and looked down at my shoes.

"Come on, I'll show you around — your cousin is working now anyway," he said.

We walked over to the site and saw what was behind the scaffolding. It just looked like a pile of stone blocks.

"Granite," the captain said, reading my mind. "Doesn't look like much yet, but we only started about six months ago. They say it's going to take five years."

He pointed over to the right.

"Your cousin is involved in the labor — moving the granite blocks and roughly shaping them."

Then he pointed to the left.

"The artists, sculptors," he said. "They do the actual artwork. When they're finished, the block is moved into place and some refinements are made."

The captain pointed again. There were two men with small chisels and hammers, working on what appeared to be the hem of Stalin's pants leg.

"Fifty-one feet tall when it's all finished," he said. "Stalin in front, and a line of ordinary citizen types behind him. Fifty-one feet tall, 72 feet wide."

It was going to be massive. Hell, it was already massive, even if you didn't consider the big concrete pedestal on which it was perched.

"Biggest statue of Stalin in the world," the captain said. "Not in Moscow, not anywhere. Biggest in the world, right here in Prague. You'll be able to see it for miles."

He walked us over to the laborers. As we approached, five faces looked up from their work. Vilem had already schooled me, and it was fortunate that Karl was distinctive-looking. As in, bald as a door knob.

I approached Karl as he stood up. I hugged him and whispered into his ear.

"The cover story is that your father has taken a bad turn," I said. "Oh, and I'm your cousin."

We walked back to Vilem and the captain. I had my arm around Karl.

"I'm so sorry, Karl," Vilem said. He handed Karl a small cloth sack and said, "Just for a change of clean clothes."

The captain nodded. He said, "As you know, it's normally 6 a.m. but you can have until noon."

Karl nodded solemnly, mouthed a "thank you." The three of us didn't talk as we walked over to the tent, and Karl stuffed almost everything he had into the sack. There were a couple of workers lounging on their cots. Nobody said anything. It didn't take two minutes, and then we were back in the car, and Vilem was explaining everything.

"How long till they figure it out?" I said.

"Well, I'm not going back to work, so they'll start looking for me in the afternoon tomorrow, maybe late morning," Vilem said. "Just calling around, calling my wife, checking my flat. She thinks I'm on an overnight, and she'll tell them that. I'm not sure if that will speed up their worries about me or slow them down — I can argue it either way. Anyway, my bosses will be in a full panic, probably by dark. As for Karl, the paperwork will get back to headquarters, probably late this afternoon. I signed it with my own name — had to make it legit when the guard asked for my ID to check it. So, when he doesn't come back by noon, they'll put two and two together by, I don't know. Again, probably by dark tomorrow."

We drove for about 15 minutes, returning to where Skippy had given me the car. He was seated on the stoop of a brownstone apartment building when I pulled up. I got out, and we stood on the sidewalk and talked.

"How'd it go?" he said.

"Fine. No problems."

"Good, good."

"And you've got a place?"

"It's actually not too bad. Kind of a shithole, but only kind of," he said.

Vilem interrupted from the back seat.

"Who is junior here?"

"He's got the place," I said.

"Where is it?"

"He knows."

"Don't you know?"

"Better that I don't."

"How do you figure?"

"This way, if they catch me, I can't give them you," I said. "And if they catch you, you can't give them me."

"But, Christ. Does he even have hair on his balls?"

At that point, Marek took the keys from me and began walking around the front of the car to the driver's side door. He acted as if he hadn't heard, but he had.

I shouted over, "He wants to know if you even have hair on your balls."

And Skippy shouted back, without even glancing toward the back seat, "Hair on my balls and a dick bigger than Godzilla, if he wants to see."

And that grin, again.

26

I knew cathedrals — the Stephansdom in Vienna, the one in Cologne, Notre-Dame in Paris. I knew cathedrals to be monstrous — in size, anyway. Definitionally gigantic. That was my belief. So, when Maria walked me through Prague to something she called the Saints Cyril and Methodius Cathedral, I was surprised. It was so much smaller than I expected. Not tiny, certainly, but more squat and wide than tall. And, well, whatever.

In Commieworld, churches were as shuttered as the government could get away with — and in Prague, they could get away with plenty. We skipped the front steps — the doors were chained shut, all held together with a comically big and rusty padlock — and walked around to the side. There was a door there, a normal door, and it appeared to be shut with boards and nails. But a closer look showed that the nails on the door jamb had been removed. The barrier was a fiction.

"Look up and down the sidewalk," Maria said, and I did. Nobody.

"Okay, quickly," she said, and I followed her inside and down a set of stairs. She flicked a switch, and the light still worked.

We were in a basement of some sort, and it smelled damp. There wasn't much down there other than some busted-up furniture. Maria kept walking through a passageway, and there was another room — smaller and darker, with only the bare bulb burning in the first room offering any assistance.

"This is a crypt," she said.

"Okay," I said.

"That opening in the wall didn't used to be there. But, well, do you know the story?"

"What story?"

"About the boys who assassinated Heydrich," Maria said.

"Nope. I'm all ears."

She asked if I knew who Heydrich was and I said, "Yes, I read the newspapers. I read them even then. I mean, I read every word of them back then. So, Heydrich, yes. One of the truly evil Nazis. Yes, the name rings a bell."

"Well, smart ass," she said. "His last big job for Uncle Adolf was as the man in charge of Czechoslovakia after the Nazis took over — keeping order, suppressing dissent, rounding up all of the Jews he could find, things like that. Every chapter of the official Nazi manual."

"He probably wrote the damn thing," I said.

"Probably. Well, anyway, these two heroic lunkheads decided to do something about it. Heroic Czech lunkheads. They sneaked into the city — there were more than two of them in the group, and some parachuted in after getting training somewhere else, I forget where. Britain, I think. They parachuted in and they hatched their plot."

"I remember somebody killed him, but not this."

"So, it wasn't hard to figure out where Heydrich lived — a big old place outside the city — and he made no secret about the route he drove in every day to the office," Maria said. "Same route, never varied, open car. And there was this one place along the route with a hairpin turn — I could show it to you later if you want — where his car slowed down to less than 10 miles an hour. And that's where the heroic lunkheads waited."

"Guns? Bombs?" I said.

"Both, I think. The details fall away over the years but, yes, both. The gun jammed, the grenade worked fine. And they got Heydrich, got him pretty clean — but they didn't quite kill him. He died a few days later of blood poisoning or some such thing, but he was still alive when they took him to the hospital. And anyway, the heroic Czech lunkheads needed a place to hide — the two who did it along with the others. Seven or eight all together. They were afraid to make a quick run for it and hoped to get out quietly in a few days or weeks. So, they hid — a couple of safe houses, moving between them at night."

Maria paused.

"In the end, they hid here," she said, sweeping an arc with her right arm. "In the crypt. Down from a passageway through the floor behind the altar — I think that was the way. The opening in that wall wasn't there back then. Anyway, they were here for a couple of weeks, but then they were betrayed by someone."

"Trapped like rats," I said.

"Pretty much. They had guns and they were able to fight off the Nazis for a while — hours, maybe a day or so, I forget. I didn't know it was happening at the time — this all comes from stories, from others. But the only way in, the small opening, they were able to shoot every time a Nazi poked his head down. It worked, for a while."

"But..."

"Trapped like rats, drowned like rats."

Maria pointed up to a barred window at the level of the crypt's very high ceiling.

"They got the fire department to pump water down from the

street level," she said. "The crypt started to flood, and they were running out of ammunition. And so, with the water rising, they killed themselves — some with cyanide, some shooting themselves."

Maria sat down on an overturned wooden crate. The telling of the story had clearly hit her, taken something out of her. Her breathing seemed normal enough, but it was like she was trying to settle her heart rate or something. You could see her concentrating, attempting to will her insides back into some kind of normalcy. After maybe 30 seconds, she appeared to be better. That's when she looked up, and made eye contact, and began crying.

"God, you knew them? Or one of them?"

"The heroic Czech lunkheads?" Maria said. "No. Didn't know them. No, not them."

27

"I can't tell you all the emotions I'm feeling right now," Maria said. "It's like they're just slamming into me, one after another. Anger. Fear. Regret. A kind of wonderment. One after another."

She stopped, wiped a tear. She held out her hand to measure its steadiness.

"Look," she said. "Shaking like an old lady in January."

Another stop. A deep breath.

"You know the anger?" she said. "You know who I'm mad at, even more than the Nazis? Lidia."

"Your sister? Did she have something to do with it all?"

"Lidia? No. We were just kids then. No, not anything to do with the heroic Czech lunkheads. No, not that. I'm mad at her about now. About what she's doing now."

"She's living her life," I said. "Her life, her choice."

"That's bullshit," Maria said. "Pure, unadulterated, intellectual bullshit. Jesus."

She stopped, looked down. Shook her head.

"My God, she's a philosophy major," Maria said. "She's a goddamned dreamer. Well, fine. I guess the world needs them, dreamers. But they're passengers. They're entitled passengers. They're never the ones that drive the bus."

"And you? You drive the bus?" I said.

"Someone fucking has to."

By that point in my life — hell, for pretty much my entire adult life — I was about as cynical and hard-bitten as they came. There wasn't a smiling face I couldn't draw a mustache on. There wasn't a rainbow I couldn't piss all over. If I didn't answer a happy story with an "on the other hand," I wasn't trying — or, maybe, wasn't drinking.

But Maria was taking hard-bitten and cynical to an Olympian level. They could award her the gold, silver and bronze just for the opening sentences — but there was a lot more after that.

"Entitled," she said. "That's the word for it. Entitled. Lidia thinks her dreams matter. That's bullshit. I don't have the luxury of dreams."

"Come on, everybody has dreams," I said.

"Like you? You have dreams?"

"Of course," I said, even though, as I thought about it, I really didn't. I mean, I hoped for a normal life but had no idea what normal meant anymore, not in the context of me. At that point, I was like a long-term prisoner who was afraid to leave jail, afraid of a world they had largely forgotten. Every time I wanted to get out of the business, I couldn't bring myself to do it. Every time I got close to a normal relationship with a woman, I allowed the work to get in the way. What did I hope for? I guess not to be afraid anymore — afraid of my life, afraid of myself. Some hope.

"Dreams? Dreams for me?" Maria said. "I have a mother who's starting to forget what day it is. And I have a father who can see it happening and is scared to death. I mean, he can't cook soup. He's never done the shopping or the cleaning. And he can see what's happening, and he not only needs me — he demands my presence. He's frightened to death that he's going to end up being the one who has to wipe her ass for her, and he can't face that. So, me. It's all on me. And fuck my dreams."

"So you do have dreams?" I said. I almost whispered the words.

"Maybe I do," she said, even more quietly. "Maybe I did. Have you ever heard of Lidice?"

I shook my head.

"It's a little town. Was a little town. Not far." She pointed vaguely to her right.

"Was?"

"It was right after Heydrich died. It was before they caught the assassins and the rest of them — before here, and the fire hoses, and the rising water. It was like he died one day and they announced it to the city the next day."

"Announced what?" I said.

"That Lidice was going to be the retribution. And they did it as they were announcing it, so people couldn't get away?"

"Did what?"

"It was only a little village, like 500 people," she said. "Nice, though. Tidy. Anyway, the Germans showed up and took all the men and all the boys over the age of 15. They took them, rounded them up, and shot them. The women and children got shoved into the back of lorries and taken to a concentration camp. We found out later that it was Chelmno. And they gassed all of them, all of the women and all but a couple of the kids who they let SS families adopt. I think about those kids sometimes, God help them."

Maria was crying again.

"The men and the boys, they just shot them. Lined them up and shot them. So, you ask about my dreams. Yes, I have dreams. I had dreams, one in particular. His name was Pavel. Pavel Kubicek. He was 17, like me. He had the warmest smile, the kindest eyes. He lived down the street from my cousins, the ones that lived in Lidice."

Full-on crying now. Gasping. Snot.

"Yeah, dreams," Maria said. "But you know what? In the end, my dreams all got drowned in the cellar. They all got shot behind the little wooden church in Lidice."

28

I t was a few nights later when I returned from my daily wander and found Skippy sitting at one of the back tables of The Eagle and nursing a beer.

"What the fuck are you doing here?"

"Relax. I wasn't followed."

"You're not smart enough to know if you were followed or not."

"I wasn't fucking followed," he said.

Jan walked over from his perch near the front. He was carrying a bottle and two glasses, as well as another beer for Skippy.

"You don't mind, do you, Marek?" Jan said.

"Fine with me."

"And I don't get a vote?" I said.

"I brought the bottle. Your vote is in the bag," Jan said.

He wasn't wrong. And besides, there wasn't much I needed to keep secret from him. I did say to Skippy, "Don't mention where you have them stashed, not to either of us. Got it?"

Skippy ran his finger along his closed lips and acted like he was locking them with a key.

I looked at Jan and said, "So, you already know about our little secret agent and his buddy from the old neighborhood?"

He nodded.

"Who told you?"

"You did, two nights ago," he said. Then he pointed at the bottle. I thought about it and remembered — it was the night Maria had taken me to the crypt. The whole thing really shook me for some reason — shook me more than I ever imagined it would. Well, for one night, anyway.

I looked at Skippy.

"So?" I said.

"I don't like how it's going with your two assholes," he said.

"Our two assholes," I said.

"Whatever."

"So what's the problem?"

"They won't stay in the fucking room is the problem," Skippy said. "And don't tell me it's because I have them stuck in a shit-hole, because I don't. They each have a bed — and if one of them snores, the couch in the living room is big."

"How'd you get the place?"

"A cousin," he said. "His wife is pregnant, and she wants to be near her mother in Plzen, so they've packed up for her eighth month and are bunking in mama's spare room. He left me the key. I'm supposed to be watering the house plants and keeping an eye on things."

He had finished his beer and grabbed the bottle from in front of Jan and poured a measure into his mug.

"Look at Marek, all grown up," I said.

"Look at Alex, still an asshole," he said.

"So, you were saying..."

"They won't stay in the goddamned room, and I think it's becoming a problem. They have places to sleep. They have a phonograph. They have a bunch of murder mysteries on the shelf.

I bring them food almost every day, twice as much as they need. I bring them beer and vodka, three times as much as they need. But they won't stay inside, and they're fucking lying about it."

"What do you mean?"

"I ask if they're staying in, and they say they are. But I've caught them twice now. They didn't see me, but twice — once in a café, once in a crowded bar. And the one of them, the childhood friend, he was fucking falling-down drunk the second time, in the bar. Who knows what they might say in that state?"

Just then, the café door opened. Three people came in, a man and two women, and took a table near the front.

"Duty calls," Jan said.

"But the bottle stays," I said.

Skippy and I talked through the problem of our wandering charges. There was only so much we could do about it short of putting a guard on the apartment door. Skippy could yell at them, but they would likely laugh in his face.

"I mean, I could yell at them," I said. "That would carry more weight. Maybe. But I really don't think that's a good idea. I really don't want to know where you have them stashed."

"I could bring them some place for a meeting with you."

"Not a bad idea, but no. That would just introduce another level of danger. If the security police have even half of a hint about me, that little meeting could get all four of us killed — or jailed and tortured. Best case, jailed and tortured. And I don't know about you, but I can't abide the thought of electrical wires being clipped onto my balls."

"The fuck?" Skippy said.

"It's my worst nightmare, Marek. I've seen the contraption — a big battery with wires clipped to the terminals on one end and two metal clips just waiting to be pinched onto your balls. Or, if you're lucky, your nipples."

Skippy shivered and poured us both a bit more.

"Where are we with the stolen car?"

"It's sorted," he said. "Stolen car hidden in a garage. Stolen plates off of an old junker. That part is done."

"And the border directions?"

"Still waiting," he said. "All I've been told is, they're putting up more wire and more guard towers every day. They're still looking for the right spot."

"You're gotten no message?"

"Nothing in three days."

"Are you fucking sure?"

"When are you going to knock it off?" Skippy said. "Yes, I'm sure. I know how to check for messages, know how to check a dead drop. I'm good at this, if you haven't noticed. But the thing is, I know that you have noticed — yet you keep fucking insulting me."

I took a long drink, then half hiccuped and half belched. I poured some more, and it just flowed out of me.

"I'm trying to fucking insult you out of this business, out of this life," I said. "You should be spending all of your time in search of places to warm that Godzilla dick, not doing this shit. It's no way to live. It's a shitty life."

"If it's such a shitty life, why are you in it? So shitty, yet you're living it."

"This isn't about me, it's about you. You think this is all so wonderful, but, well, what do you want to know? You think it's so great. I haven't had a real girlfriend since my wife died during the war. I spend months at a time living in complete shitholes. I worry every day that some country's security police are going to scoop me up and drop me into the cellar of their headquarters. And then, you know what I really worry about? What really keeps me up at night? I just told you — the thought of them attaching electrodes connected to a battery onto my balls and firing them up until I talk."

"That doesn't fucking happen."

"The hell it doesn't."

"But not to you."

"No, not yet. Not yet. But I've seen them. I'm telling you the truth — those little metal clips attached to the wires. Fuck."

I was talked out, at least for the moment, and returned to the glass in front of me. Skippy was quiet, sipping, staring down at his hands. I didn't know if I'd gotten through to him or not. I'd made an impression, clearly — but impressions can be fleeting. Lasting impact could only be measured over time, not over a glass of whatever this rocket fuel was in the bottle that Jan had brought over.

I was just staring into the distance — the table for three was engaged in some kind of quiet conversation — when I noticed Skippy look up.

"Then why do you do it?" he said.

"It's something I've been asking myself for years. And I'm not sure I've ever admitted it out loud to anybody, but the reason I'm still doing it is because I can't do anything else at this point."

"The hell..."

"Listen to me," I said. "You don't know shit about it. You don't know shit about life. But I'm telling you — you have a chance. And you need to fucking walk away while you still have that chance."

He stared at me for a good 20 seconds but said nothing. He stared, and he stood up, and he walked out of The Eagle and into the night.

29

I t was maybe two hours later. I was asleep in the storeroom, my bed pulled out of its hiding place for the night. I wasn't all the way asleep — at least, I didn't think I was — when I heard the banging.

Now, a late-night bang on the door of a shuttered café wasn't all that unusual. I had heard a few in the time I'd been there, and Jan would get up and either shoo the guy away or sell him a bottle after hours. I sometimes wondered how he decided who got shooed and who got served. Level of drunkenness, likely.

But this was different. I looked out of the small window and down into the narrow street that was really closer to being an alley than a street. How they fit the car in and managed to open the doors was an interesting feat — but that wasn't what got my attention. It was the two black trench coats that the two men were wearing as they pounded on the door and waited for Jan.

"Coming, coming," he said. I heard that shout, and I heard Jan's footsteps on the stairs, and then a muttered, "For Chrissakes." He likely figured on a pair of drunks on the other side. In about 10 seconds, he would know the truth.

Ten seconds. There was a certain amount of floor scraping in the process of moving the cot back into his hiding place, and moving the two nearby crates to cover it. In the past days, I had worked out my hiding place in case of this kind of emergency. It would be beneath the cot — a filthy and tight space but doable. The problem was moving the crates into their camouflage position while hidden beneath the cot. I had worked out the angles beforehand, and felt reasonably confident that I could get them moved.

But... ten seconds? Ten seconds before the black trench coats were inside and potentially hearing the crates scraping on the floor?

In the end, it took me about 15 seconds. I could only hope they were distracted by their conversation with Jan. Luckily for me, it was a conversation carried out at a high decibel level, at least on their end. With my ear pressed to the floor, I could hear the security police just fine. Jan, not so much.

"Unannounced search of the premises," is what I heard pretty clearly.

Jan's reply, though, was lost.

"The book says you have just the one bedroom."

Nothing of what Jan said.

Feet on the staircase. Heavy feet. They went into Jan's apartment, in and out in maybe 30 seconds.

"And what's that?"

"A store room," Jan said. I could hear him fine, seeing as how he was just outside the door.

"Open it."

"It's unlocked."

The door opened.

"Where's the light?"

"Bulb right here," Jan said. He must have been the one to switch it on, not that it mattered. I could see the floor suddenly illuminated, and I couldn't help but worry that I was being lit up as well. I was pretty sure I wasn't — I had checked it as best I could — but I couldn't be sure.

"Not a bedroom," one of the trench coats said.

"A storeroom," Jan said.

"Could be a bedroom."

"A storeroom — just look at all of this shit. When your brethren came and did the inventory, they agreed in about two seconds. I mean look at all of this crap."

Footsteps. Just one set. There was a sliver of space between two of the crates that were hiding me, and I could see the shoes that one of the security police was wearing. Beat to shit, they were. Welcome to Commieworld.

Bang. Bang. The guy didn't move any of the crates, but he was banging on the top of them. Then he half tipped one of the crates, lifting one side off of the ground. All I could think about was that it was somehow revealing me. One second. Two. Then the trench coat let the crate fall back with a thud.

"Some heavy shit in there."

"Twenty-four quarts of tomato sauce, heavy as hell," Jan said. "The delivery guys hate it when they have to bring it up those stairs."

Footsteps again. Three sets. Click. Darkness. Storeroom door slam. Muffled conversation. Front door slam. Still, I didn't move until Jan came up and told me it was all clear. And, yes, he brought a bottle that we drank in the dark. Only a few slivers of moonlight came through the louvers of the window shutter.

"The fuck?" I said.

"Not sure," Jan said.

"They didn't explain?"

"They don't tend to."

"So, really, what do you figure?"

"I mean, it's not unheard of," Jan said. "There are plenty of stories about middle-of-the-night searches. It scares the shit of out of everybody, for one thing. Just the stories — they paralyze people with fear. The Nazis did the same thing during the war. Middle-of-the-night, dark as hell, woken out of a sound sleep — it's terrorizing, the whole combination. But the thing is, they don't usually leave empty-handed. They come for a reason. But for me, they haven't been back here, not since they did the first inventory of the rooms. And they did leave empty-handed. Well, I gave them a bottle on the way out, but that was it."

I walked over and took a quick peek through the louvers. The car that had been wedged into the street was gone.

"Like I said, they come for a reason," Jan said. "The only thing they said to me on the way out was, 'Keep an eye out for anyone unusual spending a lot of time here.'"

His eyes caught my eyes and didn't let go.

"Like I said, they come for a reason," Jan said. "We can't be sure, but I have to figure that you're the reason."

We talked for a minute about how long I might be safe. We decided on a day or two, and then I would have to leave.

"And that might be pushing it," Jan said. "You can stay as long as you want — I'm fine with it. But a day or two, that should be it. Two days maximum. But, hell, you know that better than I do."

I did. I knew he was right, of course. Two days, max. After Jan left me alone, I had two main thoughts — three, if you count the question of whether or not I had pissed myself. The first was that I had wished Skippy had been there somehow, so that he could have seen just how dangerous this life was, so that he could feel the terror that I was feeling. The second thought was about Ernst. My fucking brother. If I was going to warn him about the show trial, it was going to have to be immediately.

30

Happy Heidi was not nearly as pleased to see me as she had been the first time. She looked up from her typewriter when I walked into the reception area, and it took a second for her to remember my face — but only a second. In that time, what I had believed to have been a permanent smile morphed into something much angrier. It wasn't your garden-variety, protecting-the-boss anger, either. It was worse, more personal than professional. For some reason, I concluded at that very moment that Ernst was sleeping with the help.

I started to walk toward the door to the inner office, and she said, "You can't go in there."

"The hell I can't."

I kept walking and turned the knob. She trailed me, insisting that I stop. Ernst looked up and witnessed this little scene and just looked up at the ceiling for a second.

Then, he looked down and said, "I've got it, Heidi. Thank you."

She attempted a harrumph that kind of came out as a

squeak, or maybe a squeal, and closed the door behind her with the tiniest of slams.

"So?" Ernst said.

I went to the sideboard and looked at my brother and held up an empty tumbler. It was a question that Ernst answered with, "Whatever." I poured one for each of us.

"So?" he said. "I mean, what the fuck are you doing here? I thought we said everything that needed to be said the last time."

"There's something else."

"What else? What could there be?"

"Something else," I said. "Something new. News, in fact."

"What the hell kind of news? Papa's still dead, they're still going to take the mine away from me, and you're still an entitled, ungrateful prick. I mean, stop the fucking presses."

I ignored the insult.

"There's news," I said, and then I drank.

I had worked out this much of the conversation on the early morning train from Prague to Brno, the milk run. I had gotten to the same point in a couple of different ways, but the decision after that didn't change. As in, how was I going to be able to tell Ernst that he was about to be arrested and put on trial without revealing my chosen profession?

I debated it for about half of the train ride and concluded that I was going to have to tell him the truth.

"I lied to you about what I did for a living," I said.

"Figures."

"Just shut up for, like, thirty fucking seconds," I said.

He sipped, then gave me an empty look.

"My last months in Vienna, before the Anschluss, I was working as a courier for Czech intelligence," I said.

"The fuck?"

"Just listen," I said. At which point, I laid out the pattern of my spying career — not every detail, but the highlights. How I spied for the Czechs in Zurich in the months right before the war. How I fell in love with Manon and worked with her in the French Resistance until she died. How I stayed in the Resistance through the end of the war, and how I then joined the Gehlen Org after the war.

"A Western spy?" Ernst said.

"That's pretty much it."

He drank, then shook his head, then whistled.

"So, what are you doing here?"

"In Czechoslovakia? You don't need to know that."

"No, what are you doing here in my fucking office?"

"Well, there's news," I said. "We have people with connections in the government. And, well, we have some information."

"Okay."

"It's related to you?"

"They're coming for the mine?" Ernst said. "I mean, I already knew that."

"Not that."

"Then what?"

"The news we have isn't that they're coming for the mine," I said. "The news we have is that they're coming for you."

In that second — just like Happy Heidi — Ernst's expression changed. The look he offered as I told my story had been, I don't know, kind of a bored defiance. The news that I was a spy did dent that a little, but only a little and only briefly. Other than that, the mask was in place, the mask and the face that said that he was in the right and that I was the asshole.

But then, snap. Suddenly, my brother couldn't hide the terror in his eyes.

"I mean, what does that even mean?" he said. "They're coming for me? For me? That's bullshit. They're coming for the mine."

"They might be coming for the mine but they're coming for you, too," I said.

"And how do you know?"

"We have somebody on the inside," I said. "And he has seen the list. They're about to arrest a group of people and charge them with crimes against the state, or some such thing, and your name is on the list."

He poured himself another measure. None for me. I thought I saw his hand shake, just a little bit, as he grabbed the bottle.

"You follow the trials in the papers, right?" I said.

"Some," he said.

"Bullshit."

"Okay, yeah, I follow them."

"Well, I saw one, right in the courtroom," I said. "The poor guy on trial, I don't know if he was drugged of if they'd just beaten the life out of him, but he was almost catatonic. And he read his testimony from a piece of paper and, I swear to God, whatever he really did, he admitted to ten times more. It was just crushing, all for the entertainment of the people in the court-room, all for the newspaper stories the next day. And the poor guy, I just can't even describe it. He was pathetic, the sad fuck."

Ernst tried to hide his fear but, well, the eyes. They betrayed him. He said, "Nah, your information is bad. Your guy must be mistaken." He said it with as much bravado as he could muster.

But his eyes.

"The information is good," I said. First, I had snatched the bottle from the table and poured more for both of us.

"It's solid," I said. "It's not like word of mouth or something that could be misinterpreted. Your name is on a piece of paper. The charges are listed on a piece of paper. It's all legit. There's no doubt about it, no chance that it's wrong. List of names, list of charges. Ernst Kovacs, on the list."

"And you've seen the actual paper?"

"No."

"Well, there you go," he said.

"There I go, what?"

"You haven't seen it. It might be bullshit."

"It's not bullshit."

"You haven't seen it. It might be."

"If I thought it was bullshit, do you really think I would have come all the way back down here after the way our last meeting ended?" I said. "I mean, Christ. 'See you in hell.' I didn't come back on some goddamned whim."

Ernst didn't say anything to that. He just sat back, sat and sipped. He was thinking, clearly, calculating — and his face was impassive. When he finally spoke, he said, "I can take care of myself."

But his eyes.

31

The whole purpose of the trip had been to offer Ernst a way out. But as I sat there, absorbing his bitter bile, I was having trouble pulling the trigger. Maybe I didn't have to hold his hand across the border after all. Maybe warning him would be enough.

I mean, of course it wasn't, but it was something. The warning was more than he deserved. And besides, he might not need my help getting out. Ernst was a weasel, and he could very well have his own weaselly way out. I'm sure he had a car and access to petrol, and he knew where the border was as well as I did. I'm sure he had some money squirreled away, and unless the border was currently being staffed by robots, a wad of cash put in the proper hands could almost certainly result in a man working the border taking a smoke break for five minutes. For the right five minutes.

I can take care of myself.

He said that, and then we just sat there. I was suddenly wondering about his wife and kids. For some reason, I had never figured them into the calculus of escaping over the border. But there was just no way — seven people in total, including a woman, a 12-year-old and a 10-year-old. It was impossible.

"Your family," I said.

"They're gone."

"What do you mean, gone?"

"Gone as in fucking gone. Gone as in gone to her mother's house for over a year. Eighteen months. That kind of gone."

I thought for a second and said, "So, did she catch you fucking Happy Heidi?"

Ernst blushed.

"Educated guess," I said.

"Right on the desk," he said. Half a laugh, bitter more than funny. Long, long sip.

"Her bare ass cheeks on the desk? The almighty desk? Tell me it was on Papa's side. Please. Tell me the bare ass cheeks left a mark."

"Fuck you," he said. Another half a laugh. Another drink. Then, silence. Then, the quickest hint of a tear on his right cheek, flicked away by his finger.

And then Ernst cleared his throat and croaked out the six words that I somehow knew were coming all along.

Six words:

"Can you help me get out?"

"That's why I came, I said.

Ernst began crying. Big, fat tears. Heaving chest. Snot. The whole thing.

"I've been embezzling from the company ever since the Nazis left," he said. "I can't cook a fucking egg, but I can cook the books. And I've been able to siphon off about 10 percent of the profits for the last five years. It's a decent sum."

"And where is it?"

"Switzerland."

I whistled.

"And that is..."

"That is very fucking illegal in this particular Communist workers' paradise," Ernst said. "That is, in the parlance, a crime against the people. At least, I'm pretty sure it is."

"And they must know at this point."

"I would guess," he said. "I mean, I'm pretty sure they can't touch the money — the Swiss bankers are handy that way."

"How have you been making the deposits?"

"I've been paying a guy. He gets 20 percent and moves 80 percent to Zurich. I guess they got to him."

He had wiped his face and recovered during the explanation. But then Ernst stopped, and he drank, and he began crying all over again. Seeing as how his sleeve was drenched, I looked around the office and spotted a tea towel on the sideboard. I walked over, picked it up, and tossed it to him.

Wipe, wipe.

"You know who taught me, right?" he said.

"Taught you what?"

"Taught me about the fine art of embezzling."

My father. Christ.

"That proper, stick-up-his-ass—"

"Yeah, him," Ernst said.

I was stunned.

"A grand Kovacs family tradition, passed down from father to son," he said. "Grandpapa taught him, and he taught me."

Grandpapa. The other proper, stick-up-his-ass... The father who drove Uncle Otto out of Brno, just as my father drove me out.

"Remember what Papa always said?"

"He said a lot of shit, I don't know," I said.

"About the business, I mean."

"No, tell me."

"Sure, you remember," Ernst said. "He'd be talking at dinner — he said it a million times. About the books."

I didn't remember but then I did. I could see him sitting there at the head of the table, Mother at the other end. Dressed for dinner, always in a coat and tie. Us, too. And he'd be lecturing and jabbing at the air while holding his fork like a professor with a pointer, or maybe like a conductor with a baton.

I closed my eyes for a second and saw him waving that fork, and then I blurted it out:

Control of the books is control of the business.

"Exactly," Ernst said. "'Control of the books is control of the business.' He had the first Swiss bank account. I just took it over after he died."

"How did you do it?"

"He was the most prominent client of the First Bank of Brno," he said. "The bank president took care of the transfers personally. Even after the Nazis came."

"He embezzled from the Nazis? No wonder he fucking drank himself to death."

"It wasn't that hard," Ernst said. He walked over to the desk, the almighty desk, and grabbed a handful of papers from the bottom left drawer.

"Phony invoices," he said, tossing them on the table in front of me. "We have a friendly printer who takes care of them."

I riffled through the stack. Machine repair company. Lubricating oil. An accountancy firm.

"A fake accountant?" I said.

"Who performed fake annual audits," Ernst said. "He was good, the old man. Never a hint of trouble from the tax people. Not a whiff."

"But then..."

"Yeah, but then the Communists," he said. "Transferring funds to a Swiss bank account became verboten. The old man at the First Bank said he was out. But the old man has a son who works in the office next door, and he was willing—"

"For a 20 percent cut of the action—"

"To continue moving the money," Ernst said. "If I had to guess, that's where I've gotten caught."

"Must be a pretty big bank account in Zurich at this point."

"You couldn't imagine."

"Ten percent of everything, since time immemorial?"

"Since they put the first shovel in the ground in the 1870s."

"But it's never been touched?" I said. "I mean, what was the goddamn point if the money was never going to be spent on anything?"

"Security," Ernst said.

"Bullshit. The Nazis came, and the two of you stayed even with a pile of money in Zurich waiting for you. The Communists came, and you stayed. I mean, you could have gotten out at the beginning. Security my ass. It was just a sport. You did it just because you could, and so did Papa, and so did Grandpapa. You all just had to prove to yourselves just how fucking clever you were, so much more than..."

I stopped.

"More than Uncle Otto and you?" Ernst said. "Is that what you're thinking? Well, it's not all about you. It never was."

And there we were, back to the bitter bile. Part of me wanted to walk away. A big part of me. I had done my requisite duty as a brother, and I could live with whatever happened after that. I really thought I could.

But then, I don't know.

"Do you have a car and enough petrol to get us to Prague?" I said.

Ernst nodded.

"Do we have to bring Happy Heidi?"

"Hell, no," he said.

"If we stop at your house, it's for one small bag and five minutes tops. Even that's a risk, but maybe not so much. If they were to arrest you during the day, they'd come here to the office."

"Why haven't they done it yet?"

"Paperwork," I said. "Apparently, even in the creation of fiction, they insist on the paperwork being just so."

Ernst nodded. I drove as he pointed out the directions. The house was nothing special, not ramshackle but in need of a paint job, if nothing else. Cheap bastard. He was in and out in four minutes.

PART IV

32

A lex was on the phone with his mother. The connection was unusually clear — no static, no crackling, only the occasional fade in/fade out.

It was late August. The fall term would begin in two weeks. Otto had made a phone call and there was a spot for Alex in a good school, if he wanted it. And he did want it. He wanted it more than he had ever wanted anything.

He couldn't believe how he felt, so free. He didn't get the stomach aches anymore, the ones that tended to accompany one of his father's lectures. He slept better in Vienna. He laughed harder. He knew this was the answer, and that his uncle was more than willing to take him in.

But his parents.

"It's such a big move," his mother said, for about the fifth time. In the background, Alex could picture his father coming in and out of the entrance hallway where the phone was located. He could see him pointing at his watch, reminding her that the clock was ticking on the long-distance bill. He could picture his mother, too. He could see her sitting next to the tiny telephone table, sitting on the wooden chair with the green velvet seat cushion. He could see her holding the phone to her left ear, holding the left earring she had removed in her right hand. Sometimes she put it down on the table and fiddled with it. Most times, though, she held it.

Alex and his mother had been talking for 15 minutes already, and they had gone around the same circle several times. None of this conversation was new to either of them, other than the Vienna part. They had been talking about it since he was about 12. Four years, then, of a debate that could be summed up in two sentences.

Alex: Why does he hate me?

Mother: He doesn't hate you, he just wants the best for you.

That was the underpinning of this conversation, too, even if neither of them spoke the familiar lines. They weren't necessary. They had moved beyond them.

The first conversation, the one with his father, had gone predictably horribly. It had been two days earlier, and the old man had ended up hanging up on his son — but not before he screamed into the phone, "Your place is here, Alex, not with that layabout brother of mine. Here, Alex. You're only 16. Here!" Click.

This call, the second call, was placed intentionally before his father returned home from work. But the operator had struggled with the connection and took nearly two hours to place the call. His father was already home, and Alex had been fortunate that his mother had answered.

Round and around they went. She didn't sound angry, only sad. And the thing was, Alex knew he was right, and he knew that she knew he was right. Deep down, she knew.

When she asked him, so quietly, "Tell me about the school," he knew that he had her. When she admitted, after a few minutes, that she had already spoken to Otto, and that Otto had told her, "I'll watch him, I promise," Alex knew that he had won.

But there was one more speech.

"Families aren't perfect," she said. "No family, nowhere. The only perfect families are in the movies. You really need to understand that.

There are no perfect families just like there are no perfect human beings."

"But you—" Alex said.

"No perfect families, no perfect human beings," she said, talking over him. "And it is the whole package — imperfections and all — that make a family. They are some of the cement that holds a family together, too. I know you can't understand that now, but it's true. The cement is mostly the love, but it can be more than that. The cement, the glue, the bonds — there are all kinds of metaphors and they are all true. Because family have those bonds, and they are enduring bonds. They last. They last forever."

She stopped. He could picture his father walking into the entrance hallway again. He heard her say, with her hand half covering the receiver, "Just one more minute."

"Alex," she said. "My Alex. What holds a family together, no one can pull it apart, not really. You can have problems, and separations, but you cannot completely tear the pieces away from each other."

His mother stopped again, sighed.

"Alex, have you ever heard of the phrase, 'The ties that bind'? Well, that's family. And you can't untie them, even if you want. And the distance between Vienna and Brno won't change that."

She stopped again. At the end there, Alex had sensed just the hint of a crack in her voice.

"I love you, Mother," Alex said. "And I'll be home for the holidays, this year and every year. I promise."

"I'm going to hold you to that," she said.

"And, Mother?"

"Don't worry," she said. "I'll handle your father."

33

I stashed Ernst in the storeroom at The Eagle. It was unclear who was less happy about it, Ernst or Jan.

Ernst: You've got to be fucking kidding me.

Jan: You've got to be fucking kidding me.

In the end, I told Ernst it was only for one day, tops, and that he should stop being an ungrateful prick. Then I told Jan that it was only for one day, tops, and he would be rid of both of us after that.

Both grudgingly accepted what I said. I believed it, too. One day, tops.

To set the plan in motion, I needed to contact Skippy, which meant I needed to chalk a trio of emergency X's on the base of the big black statue in Old Town Square. It was late afternoon, or early evening, or whatever, right at 6 p.m., and the two cops were staring at the astronomical clock as it did its astronomical bullshit — as was everybody else in the square. They had all gravitated over to the clock, about 50 people in all, and I was left alone by the statue. X, X, X. It didn't take five seconds, and nobody noticed me.

Which meant I had six hours to kill before heading over to

the St. Norbert statue on the bridge. There was no way in hell that I was going to attempt to entertain Ernst for that long, or listen to his self-absorbed whining. The car ride from Brno had been had enough, and we were going to have another long stretch in the car very soon, and that was plenty bad enough. We were also going to have to share the storeroom for the night and at least part of the next day, the thought of which gave me a shiver. The idea of dinner and chit-chat on top of that — no. Hell, no.

My plan was to drink. Then I turned around from the statue and ran into Skippy. Like, we literally bumped into each other.

"The fuck?" I said.

"Just checking for a signal," he said.

"Now what?"

"Come on," he said. We walked together, past the people staring at the clock, down the main street and then off into the alleys. We turned two or three times, deeper and deeper into nowhere, and ended up at a small bar. No name over the door.

We got two beers at a back table. The place was half full — all men.

"So?" Skippy said.

"Change of plans."

"The hell? I haven't been contacted yet about the border."

"Like I said, change of plans."

I laid out what I had been thinking about since I began driving from Brno with Ernst. In my head, I had thought it would be the following night. But running into Skippy meant we could do it immediately. Since there was nothing to set up, there was no reason not to go now.

Skippy listened to the plan, and had me repeat it again, just to make sure he understood it.

"So, have you been contacted?" he said.

I shook my head.

"So what's the damn emergency?"

I had debated whether to tell him, and figured I owed him that much. So, I laid out the tale of my goddamn brother and the show trials.

He whistled softly.

"So that was Fritz?"

"Yes, Fritz," I said. "He gave me the information."

"So now, all four of you? Over the border?"

"We'll fit in the car, right?"

"No problem there," Skippy said. "You could easily fit two more — three in the front, three in the back. It's a big-ass car."

"And the plates?"

"I told you, that's done. Plates from an old junker. It's gassed up and waiting."

He stopped, thought for a second.

"You know, I could just take you to the apartment now, where they're stashed," Skippy said. "It would eliminate all of this other stuff. I mean, how big a risk would it be?"

"Big enough," I said. "I mean, I don't fucking know — but to me, in the grand scheme of things, any risk is too big of a risk. That's especially true as you get toward the end. Maybe it's just a human nature thing, but I get more nervous as I get closer to the time to go. And, hell, maybe I'm being followed, maybe you're being followed, maybe the military intelligence people are getting closer to finding Vilem Novak , their wayward captain. I mean, I just don't know. This just seems safer somehow."

"But more complicated."

"Not that complicated."

"A little complicated," Skippy said. "Maybe overthinking it a little."

I didn't disagree with him. I had debated the same thing with myself.

"I get it," I said. "But if they're watching the apartment, and we do it there, we're all fucking cooked. This way is safer. At least, a little safer."

Skippy asked about where I intended to try to cross the border. I told him not to worry about it, that I had a plan. And I did have a plan, too. What I didn't tell him was that my plan was going to involve a healthy dose of improvisation at the end — heavy as in complete, total, almost lunatic improvisation. But he didn't need to know that. He might piss himself right there in the chair if I told him.

The waiter came by and we got a second beer.

"So, the place. You're sure you know it, right?"

Skippy nodded.

"So you can tell them?"

He nodded again, then said, "But are you sure they'll be able to find it?"

"They both grew up in Prague. They'll know where it is."

Skippy nodded again, sipped his beer.

"It'll work," he said.

"But you're not coming."

"The hell I'm not," he said, louder than he intended. An old guy, half asleep two tables over, roused for an instant and then his head dropped again.

"You're not coming," I said. "My boy, you listen and listen good."

"I'm not a fucking boy."

"Marek," I said. "The plan is too, well, too improvised at this point. The risks have grown a lot — not exponentially, but a lot. My brother has complicated things, and that has to be on me, not you. This isn't just business now — it's personal for me, and the personal part has added some risk, and that's my risk, not yours. The timing has been moved up. It was always going to be dangerous, and now it's more dangerous. How much more, I don't know."

"All the more reason for me to be involved," Skippy said.

"No," I said, and this time I was the one talking louder than I had expected. The same old man, two tables over, performed the same little pantomime, head rising for a second and then falling.

"More danger, more reason for some backup," Skippy said. He was hissing the words.

"No," I said. "No, and that's fucking final. You're out. I couldn't have done this without you — I know that, Fritz knows that. But, fuck it, this is where it ends. After you put them in the car, you're out. Period."

He started to say something.

"Period," I said. "And I outrank your ass, so that's an order."

34

Part of me wanted to walk to the meeting spot rather than driving Ernst's car bearing Ernst's license plate. Why take the risk, right? But the other part of me knew that Ernst would be carrying the small suitcase and bitching with every step. Also, bitching aside, a man carrying a suitcase for about 45 minutes would be more conspicuous than a man walking empty-handed, and more conspicuous was another risk. Right? So, we drove.

We left at 10:30, and the only person happier than Ernst was Jan.

"You didn't leave anything behind, right?"

"Didn't bring anything, didn't leave anything. Well, whatever I brought fit in my coat pocket."

I patted the pocket. Jan smiled.

"You are an interesting man, Alex Kovacs," he said. "Even if your brother is an asshole."

"He showed his true colors?"

"I brought him up a plate and he complained about everything on it."

"He bitched about your goulash?"

"Fucking asshole — you come from the same mother?"

"Hard even for me to believe sometimes," I said.

Jan hugged me. I thanked him.

"I was glad for the excitement," he said. "Every once in a while, you need to give your heart a little jolt just to make sure you're still alive. But, well, I think this was enough of a jolt for a while."

Once in the car, we were headed up pretty close to Prague Castle. I had seen the street on one of my walks, a street called Loretanska, and it had exactly what I was looking for — hiding places in plain sight because the sidewalk, for a couple of blocks, was actually a covered arcade. There was a kind of scalloped ceiling, which I didn't care about but which was nice to look at. The key was the series of pillars that held up the arcade, pillars along the curb that threw dark shadows and provided the expected cover besides.

The castle itself was where Heydrich's offices were, where he was headed on that morning when Maria's heroic Czech lunkheads hit his car with the bomb that eventually killed him. Maria. I knew I would never see her again, and I was fine enough with that — it was just sex, really. And if her bitching about her lot in life sounded faintly like Ernst's bitching, well, it was still different. And the difference wasn't just the sex. At least, that's what I told myself.

By then, after the Nazis, the castle had just turned into a glorified government office building — which meant that, right at 6 o'clock every night, it pretty much emptied out. Maybe the Commie bureaucrats stopped for a beer on the way home, but we were way past that. There were a handful of cars parked on the street, and the light from a couple of the cafés still spilled out of their front windows and onto the dark sidewalks, but it was only a couple — one on the first block, one on the next. Most of the cafés made their real money at lunch, after all, and shut down early. But a couple were open, and Loretanska was quiet but not completely dead. That is what I had been hoping for, and that is what we found.

I circled once in the car, saw nothing untoward, and then parked on a side street. I checked my watch. It was 10:55. Five minutes to go.

"Leave the suitcase next to the pillar — nobody will see it," I said.

"So damn dark," Ernst said.

"That's the point."

The plan, as I had laid it out to Skippy, was simple enough. Vilem and Karl were to drive to Loretanska and park. Then Vilem was to get out of the car, go under the arcade, and light a cigarette. In the darkness, the match and the cigarette would glow brightly. That would be the signal that everything was all right. I would follow by lighting a cigarette of my own if I sensed that everything was all right. If it was all good, Ernst and I would get in their car for the drive to the border. If not, Vilem would get back in the car and go — not back to the apartment, but to the St. Norbert statue on the Charles Bridge at midnight. And if that happened, well, I didn't know what the hell I would do.

"I need a piss," Ernst said, interrupting my replaying of the possibilities.

"Christ. Can't you hold it for a half-hour? We'll be out in the country by—"

"Can't."

"Jesus. Fine. Just be quick about it."

While he was pressed up against a pillar in the shadows, a car approached from ahead of us. Thank God it wasn't from the other direction because the headlights would have caught Ernst in mid-stream. Just what we didn't need, something conspicuous or memorable — and if it was a bored cop making his rounds, well...

But the pillar hid him. The car pulled over to the curb, but it sounded as if the engine was still running. It was at the end of the same block we were on, maybe 400 feet away. It was too far and too dark to see if there was a passenger along with the driver.

The driver's door opened but he didn't slam it shut when he got out. He just kind of pushed it closed, or kind of closed. Then the driver disappeared behind one of the arcade pillars.

I held my breath for a second or two, although it seemed like 20 or 30. One second, two seconds — and then there was the flash of a lit match, and then the singular glow of a cigarette being smoked, brighter and then less bright with each puff. I couldn't see his face, but it was Vilem. Had to be.

I reached into my pocket for my own matches and cigarettes. Nothing was untoward, other than Ernst taking a comically long piss accompanied by comically pleasure-filled sighs. I hissed at him, "Will you fucking finish already?" I managed to distract myself and dropped the box of matches. It took me a few seconds to bend over and retrieve them.

My hands were shaking just a little as I slid the box open and pulled out a match, which I instantly dropped. But I had the second one firmly in my hand as I closed the box and turned to strike the match on its rough side.

Then there was a shout. I couldn't make it out.

Then there was a gun shot.

Then, there was a second gun shot.

I rushed toward the blasts. I brushed against Ernst, who still had his dick in his hands, and he nearly fell over and cursed. The shots came from in front of me and from behind Vilem. I ran past their parked car and yelled, "Stay the fuck down." I assumed he heard me.

I did have a small pistol — Ernst had brought it. It had been Papa's, small enough to seem a toy but, my brother insisted, a real weapon nonetheless. He said he sometimes fired it at tin cans in a field. Said it relaxed him.

As I ran, I noticed over my shoulder that Vilem had ignored me. He had a pistol, too — likely his service revolver — and he was nearly on my shoulder as we came to a body lying in the street. It was a man, and he was dressed in civilian clothes. His hat had gone flying.

Vilem leaned down, stared at the face in the darkness. The back of the head was blown off. The man was quite dead.

"Fucking Ruger," he said.

"Fucking who?"

"Ruger. He sat at the desk next to mine. Motherfucker."

I looked up, squinted, didn't see anything else.

"Did you shoot him?" I said.

Vilem shook his head.

"Behind me," he said. "Never saw him."

I looked up the street, then down the street, then across the street, and I didn't see anything.

Vilem was about to say something and I said, "Shhh, shhh," and I tried to listen. But all I heard in the darkness was the low rumble of the engine of Vilem's car, still running. But then, well, there was something. Just the faint scratching of, well, I didn't know what.

I walked in the direction of the sound. It wasn't far away, just two pillars down from where Ruger lay in the gutter. Then I heard what was making the sound, a foot thrashing gently — if that was such a thing, thrashing gently — on the street. I could see that the foot belonged to someone who was sitting up, propped up by the pillar.

"No," I said, before I even knew for sure. "No... no..."

And then I saw.

It was Skippy.

35

He was alive. Eyes wide open.

"Where I said?"

Skippy looked down at his hands. They were pressing on his gut. Arm, leg, shoulder, even most of the upper chest — not the heart but the rest — would have been better.

"Let me do that," I said. His hands felt wet from the blood, and the clothing around the spot was soaked. The blood wasn't spurting out or anything, which I took for a good sign.

Vilem hovered over us.

"Don't just stand there — get the fucking car and bring it here."

Vilem trotted away.

"I just didn't trust him, didn't trust them," Skippy said. "Especially the other one. Just a fucking lush. All they do is go out. I mean, they went out last night. Who knows who heard what?"

"I fucking told you not to come," I said.

"You're fucking welcome," he said. And with that, a big grin filled his face.

"You know, it doesn't hurt. I mean, I really don't feel

anything. I didn't feel it when it happened and I don't feel it now. But the shot, it did knock me off my feet. But I was kind of surprised when I felt it..."

"Shh," I said.

"When I felt the blood," he said.

He was doing okay, all things considered. I was trying not to melt with the emotion I was feeling. I was trying to be like Leon, my old friend, my old newspaper friend. He always talked about how you needed to develop a sense of detachment in the midst of witnessing a tragedy. He talked about learning that, even as the cops were turning over a dead body in the gutter, it was important that the newspaper reporter keep his wits about him and observe. Dead, yes, but what color was his hair? And what kind of shoes?

That wasn't this, though. This was Skippy. Goddamn Skippy. This was a kid who should have been out drinking one too many beers and grabbing one too many girls' asses in the bar. Goddamn Skippy.

"Who was he?"

"Who?"

"The other guy," Skippy said.

"One of Vilem's co-workers from military intelligence."

"So they were on to him."

"Evidently."

"Is he?"

"Dead? Yes. You got him and you saved the four of us. Which makes you our heroic Czech lunkhead."

"You're welcome," he said. Again, the grin.

The car door slammed and Vilem was driving it slowly in our direction — more rolling it than driving, it seemed. I guessed he was afraid of getting too close somehow. It was still dark, and he wasn't using the headlights. I could hear Ernst trotting along behind.

I had no earthly idea what I was going to do. But I owed Skippy a plan, and the best I could come up with was the simplest. We would drive to a hospital. I would somehow get Skippy out to the curb and begin yelling for help while the car drove off. Vilem's instructions would be to circle the block while I somehow got Skippy the medical attention he needed. Then I would find a way to slip away before the cops — and, especially, the secret police — showed up.

"You'll have to make up a story about getting mugged or robbed or something," I said.

He nodded. I was counting on the fact that he wouldn't be able to think it all the way through, not in his condition. That is, people didn't get shot on the streets of Prague very often, I imagined. And given that there already was a dead body on the street, the idea that the two might be unrelated was...

"Wait a minute," I said. The car had pulled up and Vilem had gotten out.

"Go get your dead buddy and put his body in the trunk," I said.

"What for?"

"Just fucking do it and hurry. Really hurry."

He backed up the car and nearly clipped Ernst in the process. My brother yelped, and Vilem shouted instructions to him.

"Why?" Skippy said.

"Why pick up the other guy? Because that way, you can't be tied to him. You're just an unfortunate robbery victim."

"Smart."

"Stick with me, kid."

"I'm not a fucking kid," Skippy said. Big grin.

"No, you're not. No, you're not."

I felt my hand getting wetter from the blood and pushed harder on the wound.

He grimaced.

"I felt that a little," Skippy said. "Still not bad... just a little..."

He was fading. The words were coming more in long gasps than in sentences.

"I feel a little colder," he said.

"Shhh, shhh."

"I"m going to be okay, right?"

"You'll be in the hands of a pretty nurse in five minutes. Ten minutes, tops. Just hang with me until then."

"I want to..."

"Shhh."

"I want to say something," he said. "You know, you're wrong..."

Gasps now.

"It might be a shitty lifestyle... but it isn't a shitty life... It's an honorable life... It's a fucking noble life..."

He stopped. I felt like crying. I couldn't let him see it, though. Not then.

The car pulled up next to us.

"All set?"

"All set," Vilem said. "Now where?"

"Me and Marek in the back seat, everybody else up front," I said.

"I'm colder," Skippy said.

"Find a blanket," I said.

"I think I saw one," Vilem said.

"In the boot," Skippy said.

He coughed.

"I'm scared, Alex."

"Just let me take care of you," I said. "You're in my hands. You'll pull through. I won't give you any other fucking choice but to pull through."

A grin. Weaker, but still.

"Found it," Vilem said, brandishing the blanket.

"Give it here," I said, and then I wrapped it around Skippy's shoulders. He was shivering.

"And don't you worry... I have plenty of girlfriends," he said. "Once word got out about Godzilla..."

He stopped, coughed. Some blood flew out, and it speckled my jacket. Even in the dark, the black of that blackest night, I could see the snot and the blood, see it glinting on the fabric, lit up by the tiny sliver of the moon.

"Sorry," he said.

It was the last thing Marek said. It was just then that I realized, as I held him there in the gutter, that I didn't even know his last name.

36

napshots. Or maybe just blinks. That is all I remembered of the next few hours.

"Come on, Alex." It was Vilem, leaning down and literally prying my arms from around Skippy's shoulders. Like, I remembered what Vilem said very clearly. I also remembered feeling shitty that I was still calling him Skippy in my head. But the next couple of minutes, the ones when Skippy was lifted into the trunk to join the military security guy, I couldn't picture them at all — and I did try. I couldn't see the lifting, couldn't hear the slam of the boot, couldn't recall the act of getting into the car itself, into the back seat. Ernst was next to me, Vilem and Karl were in front, and Vilem was driving.

"Where to?" he said, turning and looking at me over his shoulder.

"Your place," I said. "Your place in the woods."

That, I remembered. It must have come to me automatically, reflexively. I knew we had to bury the bodies, and Vilem's little sylvan hideaway was the only safe place I knew. I guess that I could have asked Vilem for another idea, but I wasn't in the mood to be seeking counsel from him of from anyone.

When I looked at the map later, it must have been a two-hour drive, maybe two and a half. In that time, my fog lifted twice. Maybe three times. The one time, with Vilem in full crisis mode — smoking and farting, farting and smoking — Ernst opened his mouth to complain and I turned to him and said, "Shut the fuck up, you whiny bitch."

Then it was quiet again. For how long, I didn't know.

Skippy. Marek. I knew it wasn't my fault, but I couldn't let it go. I had done everything I could think of to talk him out of the business — lectured him, mocked him. I had done everything but handcuff him to a radiator. At some point, it was on him — and I did know that. But that knowledge did nothing to ease the ache, to salve the paralyzing gut punch. I guess because, well, because he saved our fucking lives.

Little towns we drove through? No memory. Number of cars on the road driving with us or against us? Nope. Maybe some headlights in my eyes, but that was it.

"Are you sure about this?" Vilem, looking over his shoulder. His tone suggested I hadn't heard him the first time.

"Sure about what?" I said.

"Burying them."

"The fuck you talking about?"

"We could just dump them. The animals would get them soon enough. Foxes, like that. Plenty of foxes."

"You stupid fucking idiot," I said. "The last thing we need is some park ranger or some hiker coming across them. You fool. We're burying them, and that's that."

Silence again, then. Silence and fog. We drove for, well, I really had no idea other than what the map told me later. Another hour, probably. Anyway, the next thing I remembered clearly was opening the boot of the car. I could barely look but I did.

I pulled the spade from beneath the other body.

"I can do better," Vilem said. He walked deeper into the woods and came back about five minutes later with two proper shovels.

"The fire warden has a shed," he said.

It was understood without me saying anything that Vilem would dig the hole for his asshole and I would dig the hole for Skippy.

"Graveyard is six feet deep," he said.

"Three or four will do, but an honest three or four."

"Full length?"

"No, just long enough," I said.

I attacked the dirt out of anger, out of regret, all of that. Skippy. Goddamned Skippy. As I dug, I looked up and saw Ernst sitting on one of the stumps, staring out into the darkness, seemingly fixated on nothing. Ernst. Goddamned Ernst. And that's when it hit me, that Ernst was the brother I was stuck with while Skippy was the little brother I had always wanted.

And I dug harder. It took about a half-hour before I was done — and even though I was 15 years older than Vilem, he needed an extra 10 minutes.

"Come on," I said. "No sense making the other two muss their trousers."

Vilem and I lifted his former co-worker first, carried him over to Vilem's hole, and dropped him in like he was a sack of potatoes. The bottom of the right leg was hanging out of the hole.

"Well, jam it in," I said, after we both surveyed the situation.

Vilem bent over and pushed at the right shoe.

"It's kind of stiff," he said.

"Fucking break it if you have to," I said.

After the leg was in the hole, we walked back to the boot to get Skippy. Ernst was watching us now. Karl was still in the front seat of the car, and he seemed frozen.

"Is he going to be a problem?" I said.

"What do you mean?"

"He hasn't moved. He's fucking catatonic."

"I'll snap him out of it when the time comes," Vilem said.

We carried Skippy's body over to the hole I had dug. Vilem began to swing him from his end — he was holding the legs, me the hands — readying another dropped sack of potatoes.

"No," I said. I stopped the swinging.

"Gently," I said, almost in a whisper.

We laid him in the hole, and then Vilem went back to fill in the dirt over the other guy. I kneeled down and arranged his body as best I could — on his right side, with his knees tucked under him just a bit. It was snug, but he fit fine.

I reached into his pockets, looking for anything that might identify him. Vilem had done the same thing with his guy and came up with his work identification along with a regular wallet. From the picture inside, he had a wife and two kids. Two little girls.

But Skippy had nothing. Empty pockets, a real pro. So there would be no one to tell, no parents, no siblings, no sweetheart. Well, there would be no one for me to tell — but I would explain it all to Fritz, and he would get word to whomever Skippy worked for in the Prague underground, and that person presumably would tell his family. Would tell them that their son, their brother, that he had died a hero's death.

Marek. Skippy. My little brother. Or, my son.

"I can't do it," I said, and Vilem came over to fill in the hole.

"You know this is your fucking fault, right?" I said. A seething whisper.

"I didn't do anything."

"How many nights did you two go out to the bars?"

Vilem looked at me.

"Marek saw you," I said.

"It was nothing—"

"My ass, it was nothing. If he saw you, who else saw you? You have no idea. None. And your drunken friend, how much did he run his mouth when you were in the toilet? No idea, right? And how many of the bartenders who saw you and talked to you are on the security services' payroll?"

"We didn't pay bartenders."

"You didn't, yeah. But you're military intelligence. Separate from the Czech security services, yes? A subsidiary, if you will. Separate but not exactly equal. As in, you tell them everything but you have no idea what they tell you in return."

Vilem nodded.

"So you don't know what you don't fucking know," I said.

He picked up his shovel.

"You fucking did this," I said. Then, I walked over to shut the trunk of the car, and I leaned on it, and then I threw up.

And then, I don't know, but I was a little better. I mean, I had to be better because four more lives depended on it. There was nothing I could do for Skippy but honor his sacrifice by getting the four of us out of the country in one piece. And if that was a bit of noble horseshit, it began to feel comfortable as I wrapped my arms around it and hugged it closer to my bosom.

Before we left, I had looked at a map that Jan had hidden beneath the bar. Maps were illegal under the Commies. I only had a minute but I identified two specks on that map and memorized their names — Hurka and Liba. They were towns on the Czech border with West Germany.

"Hurka and Liba — are they far?"

"Maybe another hour. Less," Vilem said.

"Do you know them?"

"A little. The only reason is my colonel was from up that way — I had to deliver some shit to his wife once. A case of cognac, some other stuff. Anyway, Hurka is nothing. There might be a post office. I mean, really nothing. Liba is a little bigger, a few hundred people now, probably. More before they kicked out the Germans after the war but just a few hundred now. Still, it's small — a little hotel, bar, café, some other shit. Not big, but something."

"That's the one we want, Liba."

"Not the quieter one?"

"No. We want Liba."

Vilem shrugged.

"Now?"

"No," I said. "Tomorrow. Tomorrow night. We leave here about 8 o'clock."

For some reason, after everything, I slept fine in the back seat. When I woke up, Ernst and I were leaning on each other, shoulder to shoulder.

37

We were driving through Liba at a little after 9 the next night. It didn't take 30 seconds to see the highlights and the lowlights. Really, there were two blocks of lights in the whole place — hotel, post office, general store on one side; bar, café, clothing store, bar on the other side. There was a church on a third block, but it was dark. The people all live on farms and in the hills.

After seeing the sights, we turned around and found another clearing where we could park the car so it would be hidden from the road. It was maybe a quarter-mile from the town, and it was the first of the risks we would be taking. Not knowing anything about Liba, it was impossible to know who else might use this clearing for whatever, or whose land it might be on. It seemed like public land — really close to the road, after all, but nicely hidden — but, well, who knew? And we were probably going to be spending 24 hours there.

After we parked, I walked out to the road and assured myself that the hiding spot was, indeed, hidden. Then I told them I would be walking into the town — alone.

"You sure about his?" Ernst said.

"I am."

"But alone?"

"I've done this before," I said. "So, yes, alone."

I had done enough night traveling in my life to know that decades and probably centuries before the Communist and the Nazis, there had been commerce being practiced in secret along these borders. Commerce, as in the smuggling of goods and sometimes people. Really, for as long as there had been borders.

It was an industry that grew up in these little border towns, skills and secrets passed down through the generations, second jobs that could end up being more lucrative than the cow-milking and the factory shifts that were theoretically the family's true source of income.

I had done it in Innsbruck, crossing between Austria and Italy soon after the war ended, but there was a universality to the dance that led up to the crossing. At least, I hoped there was. This was the second risk and maybe the biggest risk — because of the whole Czech secret police element. Would they bother to have a bartender in a tiny border town on the payroll? Or, even if the security service was using the bartenders, would the historical (and lucrative) tie between the townspeople and the illegal smuggling business mitigate the risk? Whatever. It was a chance I had to take.

"And if you don't come back?" Vilem said.

"Then you're on our own."

"Meaning what exactly?"

I spoke the next words slowly:

"Meaning you're fucking on your own."

"But, but..." Ernst said. Blithering.

"This was never going to be a Cook's tour of western Czechoslovakia — no room service, no chocolates on the pillow," I said. "Idiot."

There was nobody on the streets as I arrived into town. My

next question: which of the two bars? Actually, there was another question: how could such a dumpy-ass little town support a café and two bars, but only one tiny church. And, well, God bless alcohol.

The café was dark, closed. Light, though, spilled out onto the sidewalk through the front window of both bars — not a lot of light but enough. I was able to peer into the first bar and check out the clientele. It was exclusively couples. I thought for a second — it was Friday night so, sure. Four couples, to be precise — two at the bar and two at the half-dozen tables. And, well, pass.

I walked into the second bar and immediately saw the possibilities. It was bigger and a little darker, and the customers were all men, as best as I could tell. The barstools were about half taken, eight men scattered along the row — two pairs of men chatting plus four solitary practitioners of the ancient sport of getting drunk. At least two of those four appeared to have acquired their professional certification along the way. There were another dozen people scattered around the tables, including a big table at the back where six men sat and talked loudly.

I sat at the bar and ordered a beer. I drank it quickly and then another. When the bartender brought my third beer, I made the inquiry.

"The border's close, right?" I said.

"Three or four miles or so." He pointed vaguely with his right hand.

"I bet you could tell some stories."

The bartender's eyes narrowed.

"Where are you from?" he said.

"Brno."

"Thought so. Odd accent, though."

I shrugged. He left to take care of some glasses that suddenly needed washing, although I wasn't positive it was quite as urgent a task as he made it out to be. He avoided me until my glass was empty again, at which point he made eye contact and I nodded.

He refilled the glass and I said, "The thing is, with the border right there, I'm reminded that I have a bit of shipping business that I need to be conducting."

His eyes narrowed again. I reached into my pocket and laid two bills on the bar. They soaked up some of the sweat from the glasses and the beer spillage, but they were still quite spendable. They likely totaled a week's wages for my man wearing a dish towel tucked into his trousers as an apron.

"Just an introduction to the right people," I said.

He scooped up the bills with one hand and wiped down the bar with the other. He said nothing, but his acceptance of the money meant I was in business.

Four beers became five, and five became six. At a certain point, when the bartender carried a small tray to pick up some empties from the big back table, he stopped for a second, leaned over, and whispered something to the guy sitting at the head of the table. Then they both looked at me, but just for a second.

Six became seven, and that's when the bartender said, "The guy at the back table will see you now."

I walked back and the others at the table scattered as I approached. Based on my experience in Innsbruck, I had expected that this wasn't the guy. Rather, that he would be the guy who I would pay for an introduction to the guy who would actually lead us across the border.

But this was a small town — Innsbruck was Vienna by comparison — and there was no middle man. It became clear that this little man, graying around the temples, was the shepherd himself. One-stop shopping, then.

"Just you, then?" he said.

"Me and three others."

"Four? Fuck me," he said. His tone suggested I was asking him to scale Mount Everest on roller skates. It was a bargaining tactic, though. I tried not to laugh in his face, which is what I felt like doing — mostly because I knew that once the bargaining commenced, the end would be in sight.

The financial dance took the better part of a half-hour — I didn't want to insult him by caving too quickly. In the end, the price was high but not too high. I had the cash, and gave him a 25 percent down payment. He had wanted 50 percent but, again, the haggling was important to maintain his respect. As it was, I was likely going to end up paying for a new barn at his farm, or a new whatever.

We shook hands.

He said, "Sig."

"Alex."

"Alex, your fellow travelers are fit, right? No old women, no children, nothing like that?"

"Four men."

"Good, good," he said. "It's not a hard journey, but you don't want anything that might slow you down."

"All good there."

"Good, good," Sig said, again.

We finished our beers and set a time and place for the meeting.

"Why not in here?" I said.

"No, no. It's a small town, but we still need to use a little discretion. There was a time, but not now. These days, I mean, you never know."

"Are these days worse than the Nazis?"

"The Nazis were a picnic compared to this bunch," Sig said.

On the way out, I asked the bartender to make me four sandwiches, and he put them in a paper sack. When I left the bar, I walked in the direction away from where the car was hidden —

just so I could get a sense of if I was being followed. As it turned out, I wasn't. I made my way back along the alley behind the café and the bars and didn't see another person. When I got back to the car hidden in the clearing, the three of them were asleep inside.

I banged on the window and they all woke up with a start.

"Room service, assholes," I said.

38

The meeting was set for 11 p.m., on the second dirt road past the church. The four of us walked into town in silence. We'd been quiet all day, mostly out of necessity — we were hiding, after all. The quiet led to napping, mostly. I know I felt pretty fresh, even that late at night.

Sig was there, waiting for us. We walked about 50 yards along the road, and then he pulled a hand-drawn map and a small torch from his pocket. Seeing as how I was already carrying my little penlight, he handed them to Vilem.

"All part of the service," Sig said.

He waited, and the silence was awkward. Then I realized what he was waiting for: the rest of the money. When I handed it over, he took the torch back and switched on the light.

"You hold it open," he said to Vilem. The rest of us gathered around in a semi-circle.

"It's crude, but the scale is close enough," Sig said. "The walk is about three miles, a little more. Because it's dark, and because the trail can be pretty rough at times—"

"Rough?" Ernst said.

"Calm down, sweetheart" Sig said. "Rough. A little over-grown. You'll be able to follow it easily enough, but you'll have to push through some branches and brush sometimes. So, it'll probably take you about two hours. Three miles, two hours — about double what it would take on a Sunday stroll along some boulevard."

"Long fucking walk," Vilem said.

"It'll be fine," I said.

"You know, if you can't do it..." Sig said.

"Yeah, yeah, we already paid the money," I said.

"Yeah, yeah," Sig said.

We all kind of looked at each other, and then Sig said, "Hold up the map again."

Which Vilem did. It really was a crude drawing, just a series of scrawled Y-shapes that led to a line at the end, a line and then a circle.

"It's really pretty easy, even in the dark," Sig said. He began tracing with his finger.

"Here's where we are now, approximately," he said. He jabbed at the paper.

"All you do is follow the main path to the big road," he said. Another jab, this time at the line at the end.

"This is drawn to scale, kind of," Sig said. "As you can see, there are three forks in the road, three decisions. Lucky for you, all three are the same decision. Always go to the left. The first one comes pretty quick, after about a half-mile or so. Get to the fork, go left. The second one is the farthest, probably about two miles after the first one. Don't give up on it. Don't think you're lost, or you missed something. Just stick with the path. The second fork is obvious when you get to it. Again, go left."

"Left, left," Ernst muttered.

Imbecile.

"The third decision comes quick — maybe another half-mile or so," Sig said. "Same as the other two, you go left."

"Left, left, left," Ernst muttered.

"Then, there's the last piece," Sig said. "You just stick with the path. Just stay straight. This is the most overgrown part, but you'll be fine. The path is there, even if there's shit growing close to the sides. Just stay on the path, and then you make your last decision when you get to the paved road. This time, go right."

"Left, left, left, right." Ernst again.

"And that's really it," Sig said. "As soon as you step on the road, you're in West Germany. Make the right turn, walk about another half-mile, and you'll come to the West German border guards' shack. Except they're American border guards."

"Wait," I said. "Where's the actual border?"

"It's about a half-mile the other way, a half-mile and a few twists and turns in the road — that's where the Czech border guards are in their shack," Sig said. "They won't be able to see you. They'll have no idea."

"They never come across the border?" I said.

"No, not actually across. Not that we've ever seen — there's a tree on a hill, and with the right binoculars, one of our men can see the shack. And they never come across. They do tip-toe up to the line, unbutton their trousers, and piss on the West German side, but that's it. And the Americans come in a jeep, come up to the actual border line for a quick visit, a few times a day. They don't acknowledge each other at all."

"So why aren't the Americans in a shack right on the other side of the border?"

"Their electricity doesn't reach that far," Sig said. "They built their shack at the end of the electric line, at the last pole. But don't worry about that — you're already in West Germany. Three lefts and then a right at the paved road. They'll welcome you with open arms. They'll make you fill out a form of some kind — they're fucking Germans, after all, although, like I said, the soldiers in the shack will be Americans — but that will be that."

With that, Sig and our money departed and the four of us began our trek into the woods. Vilem took the lead with his little torch and his map. Karl, while no longer catatonic, still had almost nothing to say. Ernst was next, continuing to emit a low-level pain-in-the-ass vibe, and then I took up the rear.

I handed my penlight to Ernst.

"Big fucking lot of use this is," he said.

"Fine, give it back."

"No, no," he said.

"Karl, don't let Vilem get more than an arm's length ahead of you. Just follow his steps. Same with you, Ernst. You follow Karl, and I'll be right on your ass."

"As ever," he said.

The first fork in the path came quickly enough, after about 20 minutes. Vilem stuck out his left arm.

"Pretty clear, yes?" he said.

"Yes," I said.

"Are you sure?" Ernst said.

"Jesus, yes I'm sure," I said.

We had walked for nearly an hour after the first fork, and it was as overgrown in spots as Sig had said. Overgrown, dark, an hour, and Ernst made for an annoying combination.

He tripped once.

"I'm hurt," he said.

"You're fucking fine," I said after I picked him up by his armpits.

"My knee, I think I'm bleeding."

"Barely tore the trousers. Builds character."

Ten minutes later, still not at the next fork, Ernst said, "I think you fucked up back at the first fork."

"Shut up, Ernst," I said.

"We've gone too far."

"I think he might be right," Karl said.

"Oh, he fucking speaks?" I said. "And you, Vilem?"

He took the torch and lit up the map and stared for a few seconds.

"Stick with it," he said.

"Correct answer," I said. "You heard Sig — it's farther than you think, just don't give up on it."

Eventually, the second fork did present itself and it was as obvious as the first. Left. The third fork came quicker, as Sig had said, and then the trail became its most overgrown. You had to walk with your arms extended in front of you to bat away the vegetation encroaching from both sides of the path.

"Is this poison ivy?" Ernst said.

"Too dark to tell," I said.

"What is the saying? Something about leaves of three?"

"Stop counting leaves and stick with Karl. He's getting too far ahead."

"If it's poison ivy..." Ernst said.

"Yeah, yeah, you can just blame me," I said. "Add it to the list."

After a few more minutes, though, the path widened and then we were there. The paved road.

"Welcome to West Germany," I said.

Vilem and Karl hugged. Ernst barely reacted.

"Left or right," he said.

"Right." Vilem, Karl, and I all chimed in simultaneously.

About 10 minutes later, we saw the guard shack. There was an American flag flying from a small pole attached to the roof. I could see that much in the moonlight. A guard with a torch, the night sentry, spotted us from about 200 feet.

"Hands up," he yelled. In Czech.

We complied. The shout woke up two other guards who came barreling out of the shack in their undershorts and carrying rifles.

39

"You heard?" Vilem said

"Yeah, Czech," I said. "I heard."

The guys with the rifles had slowed to a walk. They were about 100 feet away, walking uneasily on the road cinders in their bare feet. The guy with the torch was behind them. We were talking low, out of the sides of our mouths.

"You turned the wrong way," Ernst said.

"Shut up," I said.

"But the American flag," Vilem said.

"I know, I know," I said.

The truth was, I wasn't sure what to make of any of it. The fatalist in me was screaming that it had all gone too easily, that the entire process — from the bartender, to Sig, to the three-lefts-and-a-right — had been too seamless. Too goddamned seamless. And now this.

The rifles were upon us, and the torch was being shined into our faces, one by one.

"Are you Czechs?" the left rifle said. In English.

We nodded.

"From the woods?" the right rifle said. In English.

We nodded.

"Anybody armed?" the left rifle said.

We shook our heads.

"Not that we don't trust you," the right rifle said. At which point, the guy with the torch patted us down, one by one.

"All clean," the torch said. In heavily accented English.

"Well, welcome to fucking West Germany," the left rifle said.

"Follow us," the right rifle said.

And we did. It was going to be okay after all.

The guard shack turned out to be more than that. It was a small one-level house, with an office in the front and two bedrooms in the back. The bedrooms each had a set of bunk beds and a small writing desk.

Behind the big desk in the office, a photograph of Harry Truman hung on the wall next to some sort of military insignia. The four of us stood around the desk, and the torch guy reached into a drawer a pulled out a bunch of forms as well as a carton of cigarettes. American cigarettes. Lucky Strike.

"Anyone?" the torch said. In Czech. Vilem and Karl stuck out their hands.

"Not you two?"

Ernst and I shook our heads.

"We'll take theirs," Vilem said. The torch shrugged and handed each of them a second pack.

As he sorted the forms into piles on the desk and searched another drawer for four pens, the torch said his name was Kratky, and that he was a German who had been expelled from Czechoslovakia like hundreds of thousands of others after the war. The American military hired him to work at the border because he knew the language.

"Enough with the chit-chat, Pinky," the left rifle said. In English.

"Pinky?" I said.

"No hat when I first got here. Bad sunburn."

"Come on, Pinky," the right rifle said. In English. "Quicker they do the forms, the quicker I get back to my wet dream."

"Fill them out as best you can and sign them," Pinky said. He handed me a pile and a pen and pointed me to one of the bedrooms and Vilem to the other bedroom. Karl and Ernst worked at either side of the big desk.

The forms looked very much like the forms that had started my Czech adventure, the forms that Lidia had filled out at the Ravensburg refugee camp. Name, address, education, profession, family contacts, things like that. I filled it out as if I was Alex Kovacs, resident of Brno my whole life. I used the address of our old family home, and filled in honestly about the deaths of my parents and about my one living brother, Ernst. I said I worked at the family magnesite mine, gave myself the title of vice president.

It seemed straightforward enough until I reached the final page, a page I didn't remember from Lidia's form. They had already asked about "political affiliations." Now, on this page, they asked about the political affiliations of family members, co-workers, and friends, particularly "affiliations who might be of special interest to the non-Communist government of West Germany."

Whatever. I left it blank, signed at the bottom and went back to the main office. The other three were laboring over the document more than I did, but they were all finished within about five more minutes.

Pinky checked the signatures and nodded.

"Halle-fucking-lujah," the left rifle said.

"Back to business," the right rifle said.

The bedroom doors closed, and Pinky put the forms into four separate manila envelopes. He walked us outside and pointed left, deeper into West Germany.

"About three-quarters of a mile," he said, handing each of us our envelope. "It's a little town. That's where the main military outfit is. They're the ones who take you to Ravensburg for your actually processing into the country. We just do the paperwork here when some strays show up. Like you four. But they'll be there with a shower and a hot meal. Probably delousing, too, and then a bus to the camp."

"Three-quarters of a mile?" Ernst said. He was pointing.

"Tops," Pinky said.

We began walking.

"Well, congratulations fellas," I said.

"It really worked," Vilem said.

He and Karl were arm in arm for a second, hugging and laughing. They were about 20 feet ahead of Ernst and I.

"Well, little brother?" I said.

"Thank you," he said.

Must have killed him. Part of me was overjoyed at the humility he showed. Part of me was touched. Vilem and Karl were singing some kind of schoolyard song ahead of us. It was almost daybreak.

Two black cars approached us.

They stopped.

"Ernst Kovacs and company?" the first driver said.

"That's us," Ernst said.

"They called ahead, and we had a spare minute to come get you," he said. Ernst and I got in the first car, Vilem and Karl in the second.

They began to drive but they didn't turn around. Instead of taking us deeper into West Germany, to the small town, and the hot meal, and the delousing, they took us back to the guard shack with the American flag flying from its roof. They barely slowed down as they passed it, though. They acknowledged Pinky with a tap on the horn, and he waved in reply.

"Wait a minute," Ernst said.

"Shut it," said the front seat passenger, the one holding the pistol.

"Wait, wait—"

"You heard the man — shut it," the driver said. He, like the front seat passenger, was speaking in Czech.

40

"It sure took you guys long enough," the passenger said.

We didn't reply.

"You're the sixth—"

"Seventh," the driver said.

"Yeah, the seventh group," the passenger said. "You took at least a half-hour longer than the next slowest. Christ."

The panic on Ernst's face was apparent. I was doing my best to hide mine but I had no idea if I was succeeding. Because panic did not begin to describe what I was feeling. The ideas were flying through my head, and none of them was sticking. Flying. Just flying.

Seventh group. Sig. Fucking Sig. But the American soldiers in their undershorts. The flag on the roof. Truman. Lucky Strikes. Sig. Fucking Sig. Fuck.

We drove for about 10 more minutes and then pulled up at an old house right along the side of the road. It was actually two houses, or a house and a small hut. Both were made of stone, and the hut seemed especially close to crumbling.

"Be it ever so humble," the driver said.

The other car pulled up behind us, and we were handed off

to a two-man team — a middle-aged soldier in uniform who carried a rifle, and a younger black trench coat.

"Welcome, welcome," the trench coat said. He was handed the four manila envelopes and began walking to the smaller hut.

"Sergeant Cermak will make you comfortable, I'm sure," he said. "I have some studying to do."

He waved the envelopes in farewell and headed inside the hut. We were taken to what must have been the living room of the house, except the only furniture consisted of wooden benches that lined two of the walls.

"Have a seat," he said, and we did. "And don't think about trying to leave. The benches are bolted to the floor. The windows are nailed shut. I'll be right outside the door if you need anything, not that it will matter. Because whatever you might need, I won't have."

The sergeant exited the room but left the door open a crack. I looked over at the others. Karl was catatonic again. Ernst looked like he was going to cry. Vilem just looked scared. He farted loudly and no one said anything.

"I think we have to—" Ernst said.

"Shhhhh," I said. Then I pointed to the door, open a crack, and cupped my ear. Their faces fell, all at once. Vilem nodded.

Silence, then. What the hell. I had walked us into this, whatever this was, but I had no idea how to get us out. The security did seem a little lax — one middle-aged sergeant with one rifle, plus the black trench coat with a sidearm — but it was likely enough to stop us, or most of us. We could rush the guard, and one of us might end up getting away while the others were killed. Maybe two of us could get away. That was probably pushing it, though. One, then. And it would be pretty much one at random. The commotion of the four of us trying to overcome the guard out on the front porch would bring the trench coat in no time, followed immediately by the shooting. If we could get the sergeant into the room, though, and if we got lucky... Maybe two. Probably one.

I played with the calculus for another 30 seconds or so, and then the door opened. It was the trench coat, and he was holding the four manila envelopes.

The door surprised me, surprised everyone. Vilem farted.

"Christ, did you shit yourself?" the trench coat said.

"Just nerves," Vilem said.

"Nerves for good reason." He looked at the envelopes and told us to raise our hands when he read off our names.

"I like to be able to put a name to a face," he said.

He rearranged us so that we were all sitting on the bench on one side of the room and he was sitting on the other. Then he reshuffled the envelopes and smiled.

"I love this part," he said. The smile got bigger somehow. It didn't seem to fit with the black trench coat, and the contrast made it all the more unnerving. All I could think was that he had cables hooked up to a car battery in that little hut.

"You know what we call it? Operation Border Stone. There are people who think I shouldn't be honest about that, shouldn't tell you the story — the sergeant outside for one. But I don't see the harm. I mean, it's not like you're ever going to tell anybody. Besides, I'm just so proud of it. Not my invention, but I'm still so proud of it. I'm just bursting sometimes, need to tell somebody. So, why not you?"

I took a quick peek at Ernst. Pure terror. That one line had hit him as hard, I'm sure, as it had hit me. It's not like you're ever going to be able to tell anybody.

"Operation Border Stone," the trench coat said. "It's genius, really. What if we could lure troublemakers to the border — but a fake border, not a real one? What if we could get them there, and convince them that they were in West Germany? What if we could get them to fill out paperwork full of all kinds of helpful information and then have them sign it besides? Like a signed confession."

Karl whimpered. I heard it because he was right next to me, but I wasn't sure about anyone else.

"There, there, Karl," the trench coat said. He heard. "Yes, your paperwork was quite, how do I say this, prolific? You wrote so small so that you could fit all of your friends' names into the allotted space. But you write with a nice hand. I could read them all."

Karl whimpered again, this time louder. He began to say the word "but," but swallowed it before the time.

"I know, I know," the trench coat said. "You thought we were helping them, telling the Americans about them, hoping that the Americans might be able to get them out somehow. I know, I know."

He stopped, smiled again.

"Genius, pure genius," he said. "And the real Czech border? It's maybe five miles farther up the road, farther into what you thought was already West Germany. We have them set up in a half-dozen place so far, work like charm. Seven so far at our crossing, seven groups. And I didn't really have much to do with it."

He stopped, paused.

"Well, the Lucky Strikes, they were my idea," he said. "Hard to get but a nice touch, I believe."

The trench coat basked in the retelling of his story. We sat dumbfounded, me probably more than anyone. It really was a genius operation — diabolical genius.

"Enough of this," the trench coat said. He yelled for the sergeant.

"Vilem and Karl, you're coming with me," he said. He told the sergeant to cuff their hands behind their backs.

"As of now, these two are the prize, I think," the trench coat said. "Vilem, with your military intelligence background, and Karl, with your splendid penmanship. So many names. You two are the pick of the litter, at least for now. But I have made a telephone call to Prague about you two, the Kovacs brothers, and I'm waiting to hear back. I find it so, so interesting that Alex says he lives in Brno and is vice president of the Kovacs Mining Company, and that Ernst says he is president of the Kovacs Mining Company but doesn't know what Alex does for a living, and that Alex lives in Prague. The inconsistencies are delicious, aren't they?"

He took out his gun and pointed Vilem and Karl toward the door.

"I'll be back for you two later," the trench coat said.

"Wait, wait."

It was Ernst.

"Well, well," the trench coat said.

"I have information of value," Ernst said.

"Don't," I said, almost in a whisper.

"Delicious," the trench coat said. Then, with a flourish, he waved Ernst into line behind Vilem and Karl.

What I would always remember the most of that scene was how Ernst couldn't look at me even though he passed right next to me. How he couldn't meet my gaze, and how tall he suddenly seemed as he walked out the door with the others.

41

Ernst rejoined me quickly. Maybe five minutes. Definitely not 10. And this time, he met my gaze.

"You would have done the same thing," he said, with a defiant certainty that must have been born out of decades of resentment.

I shook my head.

"You're a fucking liar," he said. "Go ahead and tell me that you haven't been trying to scheme a way out of here that didn't include the rest of us. Go ahead. I dare you."

I shook my head again.

"You walked us into a fucking trap and now it's my fault?" he said.

"I didn't say that."

"You got us fucking caught and now you're blaming me for trying to find a way out of your pile of shit?"

Again, I shook my head. Part of me was hurt, badly hurt. Part of me felt vindicated, though. Ernst had been a pathetic weakling for his whole life, unwilling to take responsibility, morally bankrupt. I knew it when I was 16 and I knew it that day. Boy, did I know it that day.

I sat down on the bench and felt my head fall into my hands. Steady, I thought. Jump the guard, maybe jump him right now while the trench coat was occupied with Vilem and Karl. Waiting was not an option, I didn't think. Time was not on our side, especially if the return phone call came from Prague, the one that said Ernst was about to be arrested for crimes against the people, or some such thing.

"So, what exactly did you tell them?" I said.

Ernst sat on the opposite bench.

"Pretty much everything," he said.

"Meaning what?"

"Meaning that you're a spy for the Brits, or whoever, and that you were here spying, and that Vilem gave you information, and that you were sneaking me out along with the others because I had money hidden in Switzerland."

"You child," I said. "You stupid goddamned child."

Armed with that bit of knowledge, the trench coat was likely working over Vilem at that point, at least verbally. Whatever his level of distraction might be, it probably wouldn't get any higher than it would in the next few minutes.

I looked over. The door was still cracked. The sergeant was sitting with his legs crossed and the rifle lay on his lap. I could see his one shoe and the last six inches of the rifle barrel through the crack.

"I didn't have to take you, you know," I said.

"I wish you hadn't."

"You begged for my help."

"You said you could handle it."

"I didn't promise anything."

"And you didn't fucking deliver anything."

"I could have just left you," I said. "I almost did. I almost left you in your office in Brno, left you to figure it out for yourself. But I didn't."

I stopped.

"Families," I said.

I went quiet. He went quiet. The clock ticked in my head. The crack of the door showed the same thing, a crossed leg and the end of the rifle barrel.

"You know you're an idiot, don't you?" I said.

"I bought my way out."

"You didn't buy shit."

"I gave them you and I offered him the money from Switzerland. I bought plenty. If he's as greedy as the average Czech, I bought plenty."

"You'll find out soon enough," I said.

"No, you'll find out."

"No, you'll find out. I mean, you've fucked me. I took the risk of taking you over the border, and you've fucked me good and proper. So, thanks to me. But you're just as fucked. You're still on their list, you enemy of the state. He already made his phone call to Prague before you spilled the beans — and you're on a list with the big hitters. Some captain in the ass-end of the country can't countermand an arrest warrant drawn up by the leaders of the party — no matter how much money you offered him. He called already. He can't un-call. His bosses know that he has you in custody. Whatever you think you bought by giving them me, well, it's worthless. Your next stop is a show trial. You'll never see Brno again."

"You don't know that," Ernst said. Quiet defiance.

"Think about it, idiot. Tell me how I'm wrong."

"You're wrong," he said. Even quieter.

Ten seconds. Twenty. I knew it was time, that it might be past time. The whole thing was a blur after that, except for the beginning. I stood up, walked over next to the door, and pressed my body against the wall. Then I began shouting, loud enough but hopefully not so loud as to reach the hut.

Shouting:

"I'm going to fucking kill you. You ungrateful piece of shit. You deserve to fucking die. You..."

I could hear the sergeant scramble to his feet. When he burst through the door, I lunged at Ernst. The guard attempted to clock me with the butt of the rifle. I managed to duck, and the rifle butt got Ernst right between the eyes. He was dazed, and went down hard.

In the split second where both the sergeant and I were watching Ernst fall, I reached for the rifle and somehow managed to wrest it from his hands. The sergeant was on one knee after our struggle, and I swung the rifle like a club, like an American baseball bat. He went down, harder than Ernst, and his head kind of exploded on the one side. It was as if I had hit an overripe melon. If he wasn't dead, he was beginning a nap of some significance.

I held the rifle, looked at Ernst.

He cried again. He begged without begging at first, just with his eyes. He tried to stand up but couldn't, still too shaky from the blow. Then he sat there and blubbered a bunch of words between the sobs: "please... we're brothers... I was just trying to survive... we're brothers..."

I listened, and then, suddenly, I was the one who couldn't look at him anymore. I leaned over my sleeping sergeant and took the spare cartridges that were stored on his belt.

Then I stood up and I did look at Ernst.

At the pleading eyes.

At the tears.

I hesitated for a few seconds. At least, that's the way I preferred to remember it. I stopped, and I looked at Ernst, and I thought about my mother. I thought about that phone call when I was begging her to let me stay in Vienna. I thought about when she said, "No perfect families, no perfect human beings. And it is the whole package — imperfections and all — that make a family. They are some of the cement that holds a family together, too."

I thought about that, all of that. I really did. At least, I believe I really did. Again, that memory, that was my preference.

I thought about it, and I looked at Ernst one last time, and then I left him there on the floor. I took one peek over at the hut and saw nothing, nobody moving. I took one look at the road, thought for a second about taking the car, but that didn't make any sense. It was all a whirl. I ended up running the other way, away from the road and toward the woods. I hid myself just inside the tree line, maybe 150 feet away. I had a clear view of the front door of the hut.

I was about to fire a warning shot into the air.

Then:

"He's escaping!" That is what I heard Ernst shout in the second or two before I could pull the trigger. Then, again: "He's escaping."

Those words were in my head for hours after that. Maybe days. They were like the bell on an alarm clock that wouldn't stop ringing. My brother. My God. He's escaping. He's escaping.

The black trench coat rushed out of the hut. He wasn't wearing the trench coat anymore, though. He was down to his shirtsleeves but he was wearing a leather apron. I could only guess what he had been doing to Vilem and Karl.

I could see the look on his face — wild, scared.

I could see the pistol in his right hand as he ran toward the main house.

Through the sight on the rifle, from just inside the tree line, from maybe 150 feet away, I could see the bullet catch him on the side of his neck, just below his jaw.

42

"I would have fucking left him," Leon said.

"You know, I think I might have if it hadn't been for the other two," I said. "But I guess I'll never know for sure."

Of course, I did know. Deep down, I did. I told myself a lot of things over the ensuing weeks and months, but I did know. Deep down, I did. If it had just been Ernst and I, I would have left him there on the floor of the main house, dazed and pathetic.

I was back in Vienna, back at the American Bar with Leon. I had been in town for a week and already done a two-day debriefing with Fritz. A two-day, 10-drink debriefing. I extracted one promise from him: that Marek's family would know he had died a hero, died so that four others could live.

"Way ahead of you," Fritz said. This was on the second day. "I've already made contact. Did it after we talked last night. They'll know. They'll know very soon. Maybe they'll feel better about it somehow."

"It's all I keep telling myself," I said.

The part Fritz was most interested in was the Vilem part, which made sense. He asked less about the brotherly dynamics.

I mean, he knew about them, the broad-brush strokes, but he didn't pry about the details. He knew it was fucked up, and that seemed to be enough. I was grateful for that.

Leon was different, though. Leon was my best friend, my only real friend, and he had always hated Ernst. He had only met him twice, 15 years earlier, but he always hated him.

"The fat fuck," he said.

"He isn't fat anymore."

"He'll always be a fat fuck."

"He isn't," I said, barely audibly.

I tried to steer the conversation in another direction and, Leon being Leon, it wasn't all that hard when I told him that I had slept with both of the Svoboda sisters. He craved the details, as if he were an archeologist studying an unknown civilization.

"I still have you beat," he said.

"How?"

"Triplets."

"Bullshit."

"All on the same night," Leon said. "I needed a shot of some vitamin cocktail from the clinic after that."

But the story of the Svoboda sisters could only take up so much time. Then we were back to Ernst, and I guess my morose gene was more than evident. I mean, I had known Leon since we were 17.

"You're not feeling guilty about this?" he said. "You are, aren't you? For fuck's sake. Tell me you're not feeling guilty about this."

"I think I would have left him behind if it wasn't for the other two," I said. "How would you feel?"

"How would I feel? I'd be pissed off that I helped him as much as I did. I'd be furious with myself that I saved his fat ass."

"I didn't do much. He just tagged along at the end. I didn't even talk to him."

"Not a word?"

"Not a word for three days when we were in the woods," I said. "I was in the front, he was in the back, the other two were in between, and I was fine with it."

"So was he, I guess."

"I guess."

"Fat fucking coward," Leon said.

Three days in the woods, trying to find our way to the West German border, and Ernst and I really did not speak. Three days of guessing blindly about where we were, trying to follow the afternoon sun toward the west. I had only one rule after Sig had screwed us. At every other fork in the road, we went right.

On the third day, we were exhausted, filthy and starving. We came upon a farmer's field, and watched from the woods when a tractor carrying two men worked its way down a row. When they stopped for a piss, we could hear the two of them speaking in German. I took a chance, emerging from the woods to talk to them. And I actually bent over and lifted two handfuls of dirt and sifted them through my fingers when the one guy said we were in Langenau. In West Germany.

And that's where I left them. Vilem was missing the tip of his pinky, courtesy of the black trench coat, but was fine otherwise. Karl was still quiet but clearly relieved. I looked at Ernst, but he couldn't meet my gaze. And then I left.

"He couldn't even look at you, but you're the one feeling guilty?" Leon said. "What the hell is wrong with you?"

"I don't know," I said.

We drank some more, made fun of the fat guy sitting by himself in the corner, sitting on a chair that couldn't possibly hold him. We drank some more, and Leon told me about a newspaper story he'd written a few weeks earlier about a cop who arrested a guy for burglary — a burglary he only found out about because he was sleeping with the thief's wife.

"The best part was the headline," he said. "'Stolen Kisses Lead to Stolen Schnitzel.'"

"What?" I said.

"The husband robbed a butcher shop," Leon said.

It all seemed kind of normal, at least for a few minutes.

ENJOY THIS BOOK? YOU CAN REALLY HELP ME OUT.

The truth is that, even as an author who has sold more than 250,000 books, it can be hard to get readers' attention. But if you have read this far, I have yours – and I could use a favor.

Reviews from people who liked this book go a long way toward convincing future readers of its worth. It won't take five minutes of your time, but it would mean a lot to me. Long or short, it doesn't matter.

Thanks!

I hope you enjoyed *Reunion in Prague,* the 13th installment in the Alex Kovacs thriller series. I have also written books in two other series. One begins with *A Death in East Berlin* and features a protagonist named Peter Ritter, a young murder detective in East Berlin at the time of the building of the Berlin Wall. The other is the story of a Paris mob family in the late 1950s, beginning with *Conquest.*

Those books, as well as the rest of all three series, are available for purchase now. You can find the links to all of my books at https://www.amazon.com/author/richardwake.

Thanks for your interest!